TEARS IN THE EBRO

Kelvin Hughes

Copyright © 2015 Kelvin Hughes

The right of Kelvin Hughes to be identified as the author of this book has been asserted by him in accordance with the Copyright, Designs and Patents Act 1988.

All Rights Reserved.

This is a work of fiction.

All characters, names and places in this story are the product of the writer's imagination or are used fictitiously. Any resemblance to actual persons, living or dead, is purely coincidental.

For my Dad, Barry,
Who gave me my love of languages…

CHAPTER ONE
Spain, July 1938

We approached the river at dusk. It had been a terrible day. They held us back from the water although we would have liked nothing better than to dive in to refresh our dusty bodies. We sprawled on the ground, exhausted. At least now the awful heat of the afternoon, through which we had marched, was starting to dissipate. I thought I could almost feel some sort of breeze across my face, imagining that the air might be stirred just ever so slightly by the movement of the nearby river. There were a few trees their shadows long in the twilight and we embraced their shade with open arms and lay face down on the wild grass.

My feet hurt. When I recovered my breath I sat up to remove my boots. They weren't really my size. They were too big and they had rubbed my feet raw throughout the day. I had been saving a last tepid mouthful of water for an emergency, but now with the river close by, I figured that I would soon be able to refill my water bottle and so I poured it over my swollen feet. It was warm but at least it washed some of the dirt off and in my mind I imagined a sort of relief. All around me most of the men were doing the same, inspecting their feet. During the night we were going to cross the river and launch a surprise attack.

After spending time on checking the state of their feet, the more-experienced of our number began to inspect their rifles, so I did the same. I had been taught how to take it apart, to clean it and then how to put it back together again, but I didn't find anything that needed attention since it was a new weapon that I had been given only a few days before. When I had felt its surprising weight in my hands for the first time, I think that was when it had hit me that I was really in a war.

My rifle had come across the recently re-opened border with France, just as I had. All the new supplies that the Republic had received were to be used for this major attack across the River Ebro in an attempt to reunite the two parts of the Republic that remained. This was to be the big offensive that would turn the tide of the war, at least according to the Russian Commissar, who had given us a talk that morning, before we had set off on our march to the river.

We waited for food to arrive, but nothing came. Grumbling like mad, the men began to rummage through their packs searching for some long-forgotten remnant of anything that had once been edible. I had nothing. I was an eighteen year old with a voracious appetite and I had been starving since arriving in Barcelona. Anything they offered me I devoured in seconds with never a thought to save a piece of bread or a sliver of blood sausage for later. My stomach felt like it was slowly dying. It moaned like it too, and as I watched the others picking at their leftovers it howled and screamed for all it was worth. All I could do was look away. I tried to block my nose to the smell of a recently-opened tin of sardines that someone had found, just away to my right. The other new recruits were in the same position as me. I decided to have a sleep rather than listen to my stomach complaining and I rolled onto my side.

Sometime later, I was awoken by the snarling of approaching lorries. It was nearly midnight. We'd been forced to march to our positions because the lorries were being saved to transport the little wooden boats that would get us across the river. As silently as possible, although it was impossible for an army of men to be silent, we unloaded the boats and carried them over to the water's edge. I quickly dipped my water bottle in before going back to help with a second boat. When everything was ready we crouched in the darkness waiting for some sort of signal for the crossing to begin. We were going to be the first ones to attempt to get over the Ebro. We had no idea what might be waiting for us on the other side.

There was also the possibility that we were being watched from machine gun posts hidden behind the rocks and boulders that lined the far bank. We might just get halfway across before they opened up on us. I felt myself beginning to tremble, a slow trembling which I hoped that no one else would notice. Maybe everyone felt the same as me and we were all trying to hide our fear from each other.

A while later an officer of some sort arrived in a cloud of dust in a small car to find out why the attack hadn't begun. He started shouting at the top of his voice and ordered us to get a move on, so much for keeping quiet. Those of us who were in the first wave picked up our little boats and launched them onto the water holding our breath, crouching low to present a smaller target to the enemy machine gunners. The river was wide. The far bank was just a darkened blur. There was no moon. I guess that was deliberate.

As the youngest and least trustworthy of the new recruits I had been given the task of feeding out the rope that was tied to our boat, so that as soon as we were out of it the second wave could haul it back and they could cross to join us. At the front of the boat, a soldier crouched with rifle ready for action, covering the rest as we clambered aboard. There were two designated oarsmen obviously the strongest in our little group although on our starvation rations no one was really that strong any more. After the other four riflemen I squeezed into the back I fed out the rope as we inched slowly away from the safe bank towards the other one in the distance. I tried to concentrate on the task I had been given, but my ears were pricked for the first sound of enemy gunfire. Perhaps they would wait until we were half way across, or better still let us reach the far bank and kill us as we clambered out of the boat. My heart was pounding fit to burst.

I honestly can't say how long it took us to cross the Ebro that dark night. It seemed like hours but it could have been just a few minutes. Every muscle in my body was tense, every nerve on edge. I let my ears wander in a continuous circle of the different sounds that were all around hunting for something new. There was the incessant bleating of the cicadas coming equally from each bank as we reached half way, the groaning of the oarsmen and the gentle gurgle of the water as they paddled. All around us were other boats with other labouring oarsmen, but the loudest of all the sounds I remember so vividly from that night was the thumping of my heart as it tried to hammer a way out through my ribs.

Sitting right at the back as I was, I reasoned that if there was a sudden burst of gunfire I was in the best position to survive. But what if I did? What if the others were killed and I alone survived? Should I jump into the water or remain in the boat? If I jumped, should I swim for the far shore or should I head back to where I had started from? Would I be shot by my own side if I went back? That was what the Commissar had led us to believe. Anyone who turned tail and ran would be shot for cowardice he had said. I imagined him now, patrolling the Republican bank, pistol at the ready his grey eyes peering into the murky water watching for anyone who dared to return.

There was no wind, not even right out in the middle of the great river, no respite from the continual sweating which I had endured since crossing into Spain. The heat was not something I had ever known before and I didn't think I would ever get used to it. The other Brits of course suffered like I did, but even the Catalans amongst us cursed the glare of the sun and longed for shade. I should never have come, I realised that now. Now that it was too late, now that at any moment the firing might begin, now I realised that I should never have come.

I had come to find my older brother who had been missing for several months. I remember how my mother had begged him not to go, how she had aged ten years in the few minutes it had taken him to walk down the garden path, close the gate behind him for the last time and head off into town. I expected my mother to run after him, to fling her arms around him and beg him not to go, but she didn't. Instead, she went back inside to the kitchen and sat down at the table and cried for hours. I stayed on the doorstep for some time, wondering how long it would be before I could follow him. Now here I was, and now I realised how stupid he had been and how stupid I was too. I had naively thought that I could arrive in Spain, join up with the International Brigades as he had done and somehow manage to find him, perhaps in a narrow trench on some forgotten hillside or maybe in a small out of the way hospital, but I had not been given the chance. As soon as I had arrived in Barcelona I had found someone in charge and he soon got all of us new foreign arrivals loaded onto an old cattle truck and we had left the city heading for some ruined castle that was being used as a temporary barracks.

We had been given uniforms to wear in random sizes and we had frantically tried to swap anything that was too big or too small with anyone who might have something our size. But I hadn't been able to swap my boots and had been stuck with a pair that was too big. When I'd asked one of the old hands what I should do about it, he had simply told me not to worry, that I would be dead in less than a week.

They taught us how to march. They showed us how to shoot. They gave us confusing talks about the Cause and told us to hate the Fascist enemy, and twice a day we were fed watery vegetable soup that smelt like it came from the latrines. The first time I had eaten it I had wanted to be sick, but I had sat very still for a long time afterwards and somehow managed to keep it inside. After a week I had got used to it. In the last twenty-four hours my stomach had been begging for it as if it were the finest dish at the end of some great banquet. Occasionally, we had been given a small loaf of bread made from leftovers scraped up from the bakery floor or so it seemed. They were burnt hard as rocks with assorted grains and the odd nail or splinter of wood thrown in, but for us this was a luxury. I knew now that I should have saved one or two for leaner times, that way I wouldn't be setting off into battle for the first time on an empty stomach.

As we approached the far bank I dipped my hand into the warm river and pulled a handful of water up to my mouth. I did it again several times until I was no longer thirsty and then I threw a handful into my face and patted my wet hand to the back of my neck. I noticed that one of the boys in front of me was weeping silently, his tears falling into the water. Tears in the Ebro, it was something that stuck in my mind, a scene that I would never forget.

My rope was almost gone now so I knew that soon enough we would set foot on Nationalist soil. I was scared to death already, so the thought didn't make me feel worse - it was just another confusing message going around in my head. Maybe it was the rocking of the boat or maybe it was fear, I don't know, but I started to feel a creeping nausea rising up from the pit of my stomach. I longed for solid ground beneath my feet. I had suddenly decided that I didn't want to drown in that river and I felt a panic prickle all over my body. At last we got there and the front man leapt for the bank but he missed his footing and fell back into the water with a loud splash. He surfaced quickly, spluttering and cursing and then pushed our little boat sideways against the dark earth of the riverbank. He stayed in the water and held it steady as we got out and then I watched the boat disappear back to the other side. Someone tugged at my sleeve.

"Get down you idiot," hissed a voice. I turned to face enemy territory and crouched down low just as the others were doing. I pulled my rifle off my shoulder and pointed it in the direction of some distant boulders which offered perfect cover for anyone who might be waiting. I felt as if we were being watched, as if the darkness was populated by a thousand dark eyes.

Once the boats had returned with a second group we cautiously moved away from the water. Our instructions were to form a perimeter in case the Nationalists attacked, it was important to buy time to get as many men and supplies across as possible before daylight. We had been lucky here in this forgotten sector, but I wondered how things were going at other crossing points. Surely a whole army couldn't cross a river and go unnoticed? Somewhere there must have been an alert sentry to cry out a warning.

It was possible that the Fascists thought that the Republic was now incapable of launching a major offensive and had relaxed their guard. I knew from what I had read in the newspapers before I left England that the Spanish Republic was slowly being ground into the dust. That was why I had thought it so important to find my brother and bring him home before the war was finally lost. He might not be aware just how terrible the situation was, after all, the Commissars did a fine job of telling the troops that everything was going according to plan and that a final victory was still possible. If we were suffering from lack of food and many were forced to carry obsolete weapons without the proper ammunition at least we should take comfort from the thought that the other side were worse off than we were. I knew this wasn't true, perhaps everyone did, but no one said anything. Men who complained or doubted the final victory tended to disappear all of a sudden and were never seen again. I'd been told to keep my thoughts inside my head and my mouth firmly shut, which I did. All foreigners in Spain were viewed with suspicion.

Foreigners had arrived in Spain from all over the world to fight against Fascism. They had been grouped together to form the International Brigades, and their introduction had helped to save Madrid which was surrounded by the Rebels on three sides not long after the start of the war. Ever since, Madrid had remained defiant. The rest of the Republican zone had gradually been reduced. After the loss of the Basque region just two distinct areas remained; the corridor from Madrid down to Valencia and the Region of Cataluña. The two areas were now no longer connected since the Nationalists had driven a wedge between them and reached the coast. The attack across the Ebro was designed to reunite the two areas once again. It was a daring and forlorn plan.

We waited amongst the boulders for daylight. Once it was light, aircraft would be up and any element of surprise would be gone. I knew from the noise behind me at the river that the boats were still bringing people across. Some of the new arrivals came with sacks of bread and we mobbed them. I managed to get a small black loaf and before I could help myself I had devoured half of it. With all the self control I could muster I somehow prevented myself from finishing it in one go. I slipped it into my pocket for later. Soon afterwards we were off, creeping forward as the sun rose to torment us once more.

CHAPTER TWO

The terrain on the other side of the Ebro was not much different from our side, just rocky outcrops and sparse vegetation. There were plenty of places to hide a machine gun nest and we advanced cautiously with our nerves on edge. Every now and then someone at the front would give the alarm and we would instantly scatter to find cover. If there was none available we simply flattened ourselves into the dusty ground as best we could.

This happened a lot in the first hour we were in enemy territory and every unexpected sound or movement scared the life out of us. As the morning wore on there were fewer false alarms. We halted at midday to find some shade and waited for the heat to die away before moving on again in the afternoon. I remember lying in a thin strip of grey shadow curled around the base of a large boulder. I longed for something cool to rub against my face which had been burning all morning.

The cicadas kept up a constant barrage of noise rebounding off the rocks and resonating through our bodies. There were ants ten times bigger than I had ever seen before and flies, thousands of flies that homed in on us from miles around. It was a miserable time, but at least we weren't advancing through the heat any more.

Before we set off again in the afternoon I had a little drink of tepid water from my bottle and ate a mouthful of the bread I had saved. It was as hard as eating one of the rocks from the path ahead of us, but it was all I had. Within minutes my shirt was stuck to my back with sweat as it had been all morning. The men who had been in Spain longer might take their shirts off, but my body was so white that I didn't dare.

I had a cloth cap on my head which offered no protection at all for my face. There didn't seem to be any official headgear in our little group. Some had managed to beg, steal or borrow a wide-brimmed hat from somewhere in an olive-green colour, but there were many who had black berets. Some wore nothing at all, but they were the ones with a thick shock of hair who probably thought they didn't need anything. I found myself thinking a terrible thing – longing for one of those with a wide-brimmed hat to get killed so that I could have it.

It was late afternoon that we finally stumbled into the battle. By this stage I was exhausted and was no longer looking where I was going. Head down to protect my burning face I walked straight into the back of the boy in front of me. All of us new youngsters were towards the back. I was about to hurl abuse at him when suddenly a shot rang out, he dropped his rifle and fell forward clutching his throat. This was my first sight of a casualty and I looked down at him with disbelief as he tried to squeeze his wound to stem the flow of blood escaping through his fingers. I remember the white of his hand, the red of his blood and the startled look on his face. Another shot rang out and fortunately self-preservation kicked in and I dived for cover behind some rocks.

I didn't know what to do so I just lay there waiting. From nearby came the sound of rifles which meant some of our men were returning fire. A machine gun opened up somewhere ahead, its staccato sound bouncing off the rocks that lined the little gully through which we had been walking. I kept my head down waiting for my heart beat to slow and for my body to stop shaking uncontrollably. I took deep breaths and willed myself not to be scared. I wanted to raise my rifle and fire at the enemy but I wouldn't have been able to hit anything.

After a few minutes, there was a muffled explosion followed by some quick bursts of rifle fire and then someone shouted that it was safe to continue. I got slowly to my feet, half afraid that the machine gun would open up again. Dusting myself off I tagged onto the back of our little column that was heading off once more.

We left two young men behind on that dusty track. Their bodies would be removed by those that came behind us - we weren't allowed to stop to bury the dead. I couldn't help thinking that it could so easily have been me. As we skirted a rocky outcrop I looked up and saw smoke drifting into the sky from where a grenade had wiped out the enemy machine gun nest. From now on I knew we could be shot at from anywhere and at any time. I kept my eyes up now rather than studying my boots as we waded through dust pools. I carried my rifle in my hands out in front of me rather than slung over my shoulder as it had been before. I noticed that everyone around me was doing the same. Somewhere in the distance the boom of an artillery barrage began.

Eventually, we came across a small farm with empty little fields divided up by low stone walls. The farmhouse had long been destroyed. It was obvious that the war had raged through here before. And now it was back again. We slumped to the floor. I sat with my back to a wall and closed my eyes. I saw stars floating around behind my closed eyelids. I thought maybe I was beginning to suffer from heat stroke or perhaps it was just exhaustion. I was about to fall asleep when someone kicked my right boot.

With a certain amount of difficulty I opened my eyes and saw the Captain's tall shadow up above me.

"Comrade Strachan, I understand you're fluent in Spanish, is that correct?"

"Yes, Comrade Captain," I replied weakly. Someone must have told him about how I had got all the new recruits together and transport organised at the station in Barcelona. I should have kept my big mouth shut.

"Good, I want you to go back and find out what's happening with our rations. If we don't eat tonight you can tell which ever Spanish idiot thinks he's in charge of this fucked up advance that we ain't going nowhere in the morning, understand?"

"Couldn't I get shot for saying that Comrade Captain?"

"I expect so. Now get a move on, I want you back before dark. Take someone with you," he decided and looking around he saw another youngster with his eyes shut and kicked him awake. "You'll do."

We set off back along the track down which we had advanced all afternoon. We didn't say anything my companion and I, we just hurried along as best we could trying not to drop from exhaustion. Eventually, we came across some troops scattered around under some stunted trees.

I quickly found the man in charge and asked about our rations. He gave a disinterested shrug of his shoulders and told me that nothing had arrived. I was about to inform him that we wouldn't continue to advance without food, when I noticed the Political Commissar sitting nearby obviously taking an interest in our conversation. I decided to keep my mouth shut. A half-hearted cheer suddenly went up from the men on the far side of this make-shift camp and I saw a man leading a little chain of donkeys.

"It looks like you're in luck Comrade Inglés," snarled the Commissar, "the rations have arrived."

We were given a donkey each, my young English comrade and I, and we set off hurriedly back along the trail as dusk drew in around us. The donkey I was leading was laden with two large earthenware pots of stew, whilst the other one carried two small barrels of water and a few goatskins of wine. I no longer felt so exhausted. There was a feeling of triumph spreading thorough me. I had finally made my first useful contribution to the Brigade.

When we got back to our group we were received with slaps on the back and words of high praise. It didn't seem to matter that the stew we had been given was surely going to taste like poison. Someone handed me the ladle that had been pushed into the donkey's pannier and I began to scoop each man's meagre ration into his mess tin. Finally, when everyone else had been given their share I took my own and went to sit, back against the wall, to eat. I spooned the brown liquid carefully into my mouth, trying not to touch it to my sunburnt lips because I knew it would burn like acid. It didn't taste of much, maybe ditch water with a bit of potato peel thrown in, but for once no one was complaining about the quality of the food. The two donkeys we had brought back with us stood huddled together watching us eat with suspicious eyes. Maybe they knew something about the contents of the stew that we didn't.

Once I had eaten I pulled off my boots and socks and poured the water from my canteen over my boiling feet. This was the last of the water I had taken from the Ebro, although it was possible that the two barrels we had been given had been filled from the same source. The goatskins of wine were handed around and I took a long mouthful. It tasted of the earth around us, dry and barren and sort of numbed the inside of your mouth.

As a reward for our successful food-finding mission, although I suspected that the Spanish had kept back half of what was supposed to be ours' the two of us who had gone were excused sentry duty that night. I lay my blanket on the floor and curled myself up into a tight ball. It was warm enough that the blanket was better beneath me. I'd even removed my shirt to lay it on top of the wall to let it dry out a bit. My boots and socks were up on top of the wall too. I hoped we didn't get ambushed during the night, I didn't fancy my chances of surviving a fight with no boots on.

*

All too soon I was awoken by the Captain kicking my bare foot.

"Comrade Strachan, time to take the donkeys back and see what's for breakfast. Tell them an army fights on its stomach."

"Yes, Comrade Captain," I responded sleepily. It wasn't yet dawn, but the sky was thinning from black to purple which meant sunrise wouldn't be far off. I quickly pulled on my socks which were stiff like cardboard and then my boots which were hard as cement. I grabbed my shirt and then woke the lad who had accompanied me the previous evening. I don't know whether or not I was supposed to take him with me this time, and I don't know whether or not he wanted to come, I just did it. He got up immediately without complaining, pulled on his boots and we set off leading our donkeys back towards the rear.

"Try to find out what's going on in other sectors," called out the Captain as we hurried away.

We weren't so tired now after a night of uninterrupted sleep, even the constant buzzing of mosquitoes hadn't bothered me for once. All around us the cicadas were in full voice in anticipation of the arrival of the new day. This time we talked as we scurried along through the dust. I found out that my companion was a year older than me and that he had been working in the docks in London. A couple of his older workmates had talked about joining the fight against Fascism and he had sort of tagged along. He would go back to the docks when the war was over, it didn't seem such a bad place to be now. His name was Billy and he was tall and thin just as I was.

We reached the little camp we had been to the previous evening and found the men there half awake. Some were coughing and wheezing as they choked on a first cigarette others trying to wash the dust out of their hair in a metal bucket of shared water. Suddenly there was a huge boom away in the distance and the morning barrage began.

We left the donkeys with the others in a group tied to a twisted tree that had long ago died of thirst. The Spanish Captain came to speak to us. He handed me a little home-made map which seemed to have been drawn by a child. He pointed out the river and somewhere up ahead a place where two minor roads crossed each other. There was a thin shaky line pencilled in that led to the crossroads and he told me that this was the track we had been sent down. We were to take and hold the crossroads and wait there for further orders. There were some hills sketched on the map with the name Sierra Caballs written across them, and a road skirted this high ground towards the village of Corbera de Ebro, but of course these names meant nothing to me then.

I remembered that we had been sent for bread and told the Spanish Captain that we couldn't be expected to fight on empty stomachs. He laughed and indicated a pile of sacks grouped around a tree and told me to take one. As we prepared to leave I asked about the progress of the battle. He gave a shrug of his bony shoulders.

"How the fuck should I know," he laughed. "I heard they blew a dam yesterday and flooded the river washing away some of our pontoon bridges. That means we're going to be hard pushed to get supplies and reinforcements across, but it's a war, what do you expect."

Billy and I left just as the sun was starting to rise. He carried the sack of bread as he seemed to have accepted the role of my helper even though he was older than me. Like all soldiers I was pleased to see daylight, no one liked the darkness deep in enemy territory, but of course I found myself wondering if this would be the last sunrise I ever saw. I had been told that we were to capture the crossroads on my little map, which meant that we could expect to find enemy forces there. We were just a small company, what if the enemy had a large force waiting there for us?

CHAPTER THREE

When we got back to the company camp we found everyone sitting around waiting for us. I was glad we had a sack of bread. If we had come back empty-handed we might have been torn to pieces. I grabbed a little loaf of bread and stuffed it into my pocket and went to find the Captain. He was casually shaving sitting on a low stone wall as if he was on a camping holiday rather than at the spearhead of an attack into enemy territory in the middle of a war.

He saw me approaching in the tiny mirror he was using and quickly splashed the remains of any soap from his face with water from a chipped earthenware bowl. He turned towards me and I held out the little map.

"Are these our orders?" he asked.

"Yes, Comrade Captain." I told him about the crossroads and laboured the point about the place being defended by enemy troops so that he knew it wasn't going to be a walk in the park. He looked at the childlike drawing I had given him.

"Corbera, that's where we're headed, that's our first objective, at least that's what they said in the briefing last week. Then Gandesa. Mean anything to you Comrade?"

"No, Comrade Captain."

"So where did you learn Spanish?" he wanted to know.

"My mother's Spanish," I told him.

"Is she from around here?"

"No, she's from the island of Menorca."

"I see. I'm making you my Liaison Officer by the way. I need someone who understands what's being said. Misunderstandings could prove deadly in the heat of battle."

"Yes, Comrade Captain. Thank you."

"Don't thank me, just don't get yourself killed, you're no use to me dead."

Billy came over and handed me the last loaf of bread from the sack.

"For the Captain," he whispered to me. I handed the Captain his bread and he thanked me. We filled our water bottles from the barrels that Billy and I had brought up the previous evening and then we set off down the track towards the crossroads. The little map I had brought back had not shown any indication of scale, so for all I knew the crossroads could be just around the next corner, or twenty miles away. I feared the latter and fell to the rear of the group mentally trying to prepare myself for another day of trekking through the incessant heat and dust. I found myself wondering if my mother's homeland was like this or whether her island was beautiful and lush. Billy trotted along at my side like an obedient puppy. If my ability to speak Spanish had given me a purpose in this company then Billy seemed to have latched onto the role of being my assistant. It was good to have a specific role to play and no doubt Billy thought the same.

My mother had brought me up to speak Castillian rather than her island language. She thought it would be more useful to us, but whenever she was angry or excited she always reverted to her own natural first language and so we picked it up too. It was a dialect of Catalan so I could more or less understand what the Catalans, who were mixed in with us, were saying. I didn't let on though, I just listened.

Mostly they complained about the food, as the rest of us did, or how their feet hurt, or how they longed to go home. They talked about some imagined *xicota* or girlfriend who was waiting for them, back at their village. They also complained about being stuck in one of the International Brigades. They were convinced, and they were possibly correct, that the International Brigades received the worst training and equipment, the least food, and wine that in peace time would have been sold as vinegar. The thing that worried me the most was that they were sure that we would be used as cannon fodder once the real battle started. Their collective dream was to be transferred into a regular Spanish unit like the one that was following on behind us.

*

We had been walking for about an hour when someone shouted "plane." My ears were not accustomed yet to the varying sounds of war and I couldn't make out anything other than the distant boom of the artillery and closer at hand the nerve shattering hum of the cicadas rejoicing in our suffering as the sun climbed higher. I looked up into the clear blue sky but couldn't see a thing. I wanted to see one of our planes on its way into battle. Perhaps they would strafe the troops waiting for us at the crossroads and then go on to bomb Corbera de Ebro and make our day's work a lot easier.

Suddenly, someone grabbed my arm and tugged me out of the middle of the track and off behind some rocks. Seconds later a hail of bullets tore up the path where we had been walking.

"The Captain said not to get yourself killed, remember?" said Billy panting quietly beside me. It had never occurred to me that the planes might belong to the enemy and be looking for our advanced groups. I had just assumed that they would be ours.

The plane made a second run, but we were all safely hidden behind the plentiful rocks that lined the track and the pilot turned away. When he got back to base he would report our position on the edge of the Sierra Caballs and the Fascists would come looking for us.

We trudged on, all our senses on high alert now. The rocks that lined the track grew into small hills and we followed our path as it twisted around them. It was the perfect terrain for an ambush, the enemy could be all around us and we wouldn't even know it. The sun began to torment us as midday approached. We stopped briefly for a quick breather and a mouthful of the warm water from our bottles. I hoped that we would reach the crossroads soon, if not I felt I might die in this heat which rebounded off the rocks and stung my face.

There was no respite in the afternoon as there had been the previous day. The Captain seemed determined to reach our objective as soon as possible. It hadn't looked far on the hand-drawn map and maybe that had confused him. It was also possible he thought that the pilot who had found us earlier might return with a load of bombs.

In the middle of the afternoon, with the heat reaching boiling point, our track dipped sharply downwards and we came to a narrow road. I knew that the crossroads couldn't be far ahead now. On our map the track had joined the road almost at the crossroads. We spread out in a long thin column along the road. We felt exposed now. If another plane approached it would be harder to find cover. We would have to run away from the road and into the hills away to our left.

We hadn't gone far, when the Captain gave the order for us to halt. Just up ahead I could see a small cluster of buildings overlooked by a steep hill. This must be our objective. The Captain decided to send a small group forward to assess the situation. There was no point in all of us walking into a trap.

Five men set off along the road, the rest of us waited, rifles cocked and ready. I found my heart was pounding out of control once again, and I tried taking deep breaths to steady my nerves. I noticed Billy looking decidedly nervous at my side and gave him a little half smile. He responded with a slight nod.

The five men disappeared behind the first of the buildings. Immediately, a series of shots rang out.

"Let's go boys!" shouted the Captain and we charged off up the road to help our comrades who were under attack. It had been a gruelling day's march to get this far, but suddenly all feelings of exhaustion were replaced by the need to rush into battle. There was the boom of an artillery piece from up on top of the hill that dominated the crossroads and an explosion came seconds later and the corner was torn off the building we were approaching.

We were showered with dust and our charge almost came to a complete halt. Instinctively we fanned out across the road as we rounded the corner. Two of our comrades were lying dead the other three had taken cover behind a house. We quickly looked for somewhere to shelter, I heard funny whizzing sounds all around my head and it took me a few seconds to realize that they were bullets. I jumped over a low wall and crouched down, Billy arrived a moment later. We kept our heads low. A bullet clipped one of the upper stones of the wall and sprayed a shower of tiny fragments down upon us.

I held my rifle tightly in both hands, this time I was determined to make some sort of contribution to the fighting. Billy saw my intention.

"Remember not to get yourself killed," he told me. I had been about to pop my head above the wall to see what was going on. His words made me hesitate. Another bullet hit the stones. Just then the Captain came to see us, crouching below the level of the wall as he scurried along.

"Strachan, get back to the Spanish and tell them that we're pinned down. I need them to outflank that hill and attack from behind."

"Yes, Comrade Captain." I didn't need to ask Billy to come with me I knew he would follow, so I set off back along the wall, keeping low for as far as its protection would take me. When I got to the end I knew there was nothing else to do but make a run for it. I felt Billy at my elbow. I took a deep breath, jumped up and over the wall and ran for the building which had had its corner blown out, beyond which I knew we would be out of sight. We reached safety, panting hard. The gun from on top of the hill boomed again and there was another explosion.

We headed back along the road to find the track. I was surprised at how quickly we found the Spanish Company, but they must have heard the sound of fighting and were hurrying to join in. Out of breath, I quickly tried to explain what our Captain wanted.

The Spanish set off, up into the hills to try to outflank the Fascist position. Billy and I returned back along the track to the road. As we were nearing the crossroads we heard the approaching drone of an aircraft. We both raced for cover and dived into a ditch that ran along by the road. We watched as the biplane circled slowly above the buildings where our company were fighting, and then cheered as it dropped a bomb onto the top of the hill.

Billy and I picked ourselves up and raced along the road. We had heard the explosion of the bomb and assumed that the Fascist gun position had been destroyed. As we came past the first stone building, a shot rang out and I felt something warm and wet splatter the right side of my face. I turned to see what it was and realized in horror that the bullet had torn half of Billy's head off. His body began to crumble away even though his legs still seemed to want to carry him forward. Another shot came and I felt something like a fire brand scrape across my right thigh.

I panicked. I was exposed out in the open and being shot at. I ran as best I could towards the blown out corner of the nearest building. Just as I reached the hole, a bullet exploded into the wall by my head and a piece of stone flew off and hit me above the right eye.

CHAPTER FOUR

I don't really remember too much of the hours that followed. There was a time that seemed like a dream, another time when I thought I could hear voices nearby and in between just a lot of darkness. When at last I became at least partially aware of what was going on I realised that I couldn't open my eyes, they were stuck tight. The next thing that registered was the pounding in my head and after that the burning wound across my thigh. I also noticed that my back was laying on something hard that was digging into me, but I couldn't move at all to try to alleviate the pain.

I must have passed out again. When I came to for the second time it was to register silence, a more total silence than I had ever previously known. Wherever I was, I was now completely alone. I tried to move, just slightly, to change position to ease the pain that consumed my whole body, but I couldn't.

How long I stayed that way I don't know. It could have been hours, more than likely it was a couple of days. I was finally awoken by the noise of someone moving about close at hand. Then there was a gasp. It was a gasp that sounded distinctly feminine.

"Hola," I gasped my throat as rough as sandpaper.

"Está vivo," I heard a girl's voice say, he's alive. So this wasn't heaven or hell or anywhere in between, this was still Spain and I was still unable to open my eyes. Perhaps I had been taken to a hospital away from the front.

"Help me, please," I begged.

"We should go," said a male voice, but not an adult voice, more that of a boy.

"He's hurt," came the girl's voice once more.

"I'm going," said the boy, "you stay if you want, but those soldiers might come back soon."

"It's all right, you go. I'll see if I can help him."

"Water," I begged.

"Lie still," said the girl in a soothing voice. "I'll see if I can get you something to drink."

I heard movement as they went away. Then came snatches of whispered conversation but I couldn't make out what was being said. I guessed he was probably trying to persuade her to leave me. A panic gripped me. If they left me here then I felt I would surely die. There were several minutes of silence that seemed like hours, but eventually I heard someone approaching again.

"I've got you some water," came the girl's calm voice. I felt something touch my lips and then a few drops of warm water began to leak gently into my open mouth. I swallowed as best I could and then the girl let me drink once more.

"Where are the others?" I asked.

"The soldiers have all gone," she whispered.

"They left me behind," I mumbled starting to feel sorry for myself.

"I don't expect they saw you here in this house."

"How did I get into a house?"

"I don't know."

I tried to think back over what had happened. I had been running towards the hole in a building when I had blacked out, I must have fallen inside.

"My eyes, I can't see," I told her.

"It's blood. You have a deep cut on your head. The blood has dried across your face."

She moved away from me, across the floor.

"Don't leave me, please," I called out.

"It's all right. I'm just looking for a rag or something to clean your face up a bit."

She came back to me soon enough and I heard her pouring water and then she wiped a wet rag across my eyes. It had no effect at first and I thought that maybe I had been blinded, but she repeated the process several times, pouring fresh water onto a piece of cloth. Eventually, I was able to open my left eye, but the right remained stubbornly closed. I tried to focus on the girl, but the sudden return of light made me dizzy and I quickly closed my one good eye again.

The girl carried on cleaning my face as gently as she could. She avoided my forehead which burned like hell.

I tried to open my eyes again and this time I managed to get them both open. The relief was such that I felt that I might cry. I saw the girl looking at me. Her face looked worried, as if now that I had my eyes open again, I might be a danger to her.

"Thank you," I whispered. She gave a little smile and poured some fresh water over her rag and went back to cleaning my face. I kept my eyes open watching her. She had large eyes, almond-shaped, deep brown in the shadowy light that came in through the hole in the wall of the house. She had a long thin nose that dominated her face and her dark hair was long and straight. I guessed she was about my age, maybe slightly younger.

"What's your name?" I asked.

"Julia," she said. "And yours?"

"Martin."

"You need a doctor," she stated.

"I need some food," I told her. I really felt like I was fading away, on the verge of fainting back into unconsciousness at any moment.

"I can see if there's anything left at the venta," she decided. "I think the soldiers went through it though."

She went to stand up.

"Wait, something's digging into my back, I must have fallen on it. Could you remove it?"

She looked into my eyes, trying to work out if it was a trick or something, trying to decide if I was trustworthy or not. In the end she gave in and began to reach under my back searching for whatever it was I had been lying on for so many hours. She soon found it and eased me up a bit to pull it out. I desperately tried not to cry out in pain, I didn't want to alarm her. It was a large piece of stone that must have been blown out of the wall. She let my body fall back into place, the difference was amazing. Although the floor was far from comfortable, at least I didn't have that piece of stone digging into me. She went off in search of food. I relaxed in my new-found comfort and must have dropped off to sleep.

The girl woke me a little later.

"There's no food," she said. "They've taken everything. They've blown a hole in the roof too and most of the windows are broken. My father will be devastated."

"You live at the venta?"

"Yes, but we left when the soldiers arrived."

"Where are you staying now?"

"At my aunt's house. She's got a small huerto in the hills, we're safe there."

"Did your father send you to check on the venta?"

"No, it was my idea. I came with my cousin but he's afraid of the soldiers. The Fascists killed his father last year."

"I'm not a Fascist," I told her.

"I know that," she replied, "I wouldn't help you if you were. Where are you from? You're not from here."

"I'm from England."

"England? But you speak our language."

"My mother's Spanish."

"And your mother sent you to Spain to fight for the Republica?"

"No, no. I volunteered."

"You volunteered? Are you crazy?" she asked.

I laughed a little, but it hurt a lot. I remembered I had a small loaf of bread in my pocket. I tried to move my arm to reach it, but the pain was too intense.

"Don't try to move," said the girl in alarm, "just lie still."

"There's some bread in my pocket," I told her.

She looked at me and then gently patted one of my pockets. She removed the little chunk of black bread and held it out to me. Then, realising that I couldn't take it, she broke a piece off and dropped it into my mouth. It was stale and hard but I held it in my mouth and sucked it a little to try to soften it up, but it was no use. I began to choke as the bread slipped to the back of my tongue. The girl quickly reached into my mouth and fished the bread out with her fingers.

"We need to soak it a bit first," she decided, and she dropped it into the little earthenware bowl containing the water she had brought for me to drink.

"You have some too," I told her since she looked as thin and undernourished as I was.

"It's all right, there's food at my aunt's house. The soldiers didn't go there. I'll bring you something better to eat soon."

"You mean you're going to come back?"

"I can't leave you here to die, can I?"

"I'm glad you feel that way."

"I'll see if I can get a doctor too."

"Where will you find a doctor?"

"I'll find one," she sounded so confident that I wanted to believe her. I wanted to believe that there might be a chance that I might survive.

After she had fed me half of the bread and given me another drink of water, she decided she ought to leave. Her cousin would have reached home a long time ago without her and her father would be angry. She left me the bread on the floor next to my head and my water bottle alongside it. And then she was gone and I was alone once more. I closed my eyes and dozed off despite the aching pain that racked my body.

*

It must have been evening when I woke up again properly. I guessed that because it was slightly cooler than before. I was lucky that I had fallen into the house. If I had been lying out in the sun then I would surely have died, although had I been visible, I might not have been left behind. I wondered what had happened to my company. They must have moved on along the road to Corbera de Ebro which was marked on the map that I had taken to the Captain. I wondered if they had met stiff resistance there or not. Of course I had no idea just how big a place it might be or how important it might be to the Fascists for that matter.

I waited, ears straining, for the girl to come back. Only when it began to grow dark did I give up hope. It was possible that her cousin had told her father about the wounded soldier in the house opposite the venta and he had forbidden her from coming anywhere near the place. That was understandable.

I spent a terrible night awake lying on that floor. I wished I knew what had happened to my blanket, it would have been nice to have been able to lie on it. I think it was hanging from my rifle strap when Billy and I came back, although I'm not sure. I wondered what had happened to my rifle. I couldn't see everywhere around me, but I think that had it been close at hand the girl would have seen it and given it to me. If the Fascists came back I would need it, I had heard that they didn't take kindly to foreigners who had come to their country to get mixed up in their war, unless of course they were the Germans or Italians fighting on their side. And what if the dreaded Moors came through? What then? It would be better to use my weapon to shoot myself rather than to risk being taken alive. My rifle must have fallen in the street outside when I was shot. I wondered if they had taken Billy's body away. Poor kid. I didn't even know his last name.

All through the night I heard the scurrying of rodents searching for food. I dreaded the thought of a rat gnawing at my wounds when I was completely defenceless. I tried whistling to keep them away, but my mouth was too dry. I could have tried singing along to the chirp, chirp, chirp of the cicadas that seemed to have invaded my ruined dwelling, but I didn't have the strength to sing. In the end I took to reciting some of father's war poems, mumbling quietly but increasing the volume if I thought something was coming too close.

My father was the war hero and poet Lyndon Strachan and his were the only poems I knew by heart. I wished that I could be brave like he was, but I wasn't. I'd like to say that I didn't cry out for my mother in that long dark night, but that would be a lie.

At some stage towards morning exhaustion must have crept up on me and I fell asleep.

CHAPTER FIVE

I was startled awake by the sound of someone moving the ruined door slightly to make a bigger gap to get through.

"Julia?" I asked. My head was pounding as if I had hit a wall or something.

"It's all right Martin, it's me," came the girl's voice. The relief I felt was indescribable. I had never before been so pleased to hear someone's voice. She picked her way over towards me through the remains of the smashed up furniture that littered the floor. I wondered if she had thought that she would find me dead.

She came and knelt down beside me.

"You ate the bread then," she said. I looked at my water bottle and saw that the piece of bread that had been beside it was gone.

"Rats," I told her. Still, if the bread had stopped them from gnawing at my face then it was better that they had taken it.

"Rats? How awful."

"I'm glad to see you," I told her. She smiled. She had a nice smile. She showed me a little basket and began to extract the things she had brought. She had a small bowl of lentils, brown and mushy and smelling of chorizo. She took a little spoon to feed me. I tried to raise myself up. Seeing that I was having difficulty she put her hand behind my neck and helped me lift my head just slightly and then she spooned the lentils into my mouth. I had eaten lentils at home before, many times, my mother had always cooked in a Spanish style, but even cooked the previous day and cold it was far and away the best dish of lentils I had ever had. And of course, from that day onwards whenever I ate lentils I always thought of Julia and that bombed out house opposite the venta.

After a couple of spoonfuls of lentils she gave me a drink of water from a glass bottle which was plugged with a cork. She told me that the water came from the well in her aunt's little orchard and it certainly tasted fresh and almost cool. I wanted more food, but she said I shouldn't eat too much in one go, not having been near starvation as I had been over the last few weeks.

She bathed my head with some of the fresh water and a clean-looking cloth and then produced a small brown bottle containing some liquid.

"I didn't manage to bring a doctor, but I found this. It might smart a bit," she said, "close your eyes."

I closed my eyes. She poured a few drops of the liquid onto the wound above my right eye. I cried out in shock and surprise. I don't know what that liquid was, and she never told me, but it burnt like acid. I tried not to cry like a baby, but it really stung. She said it would make sure that the wound didn't get infected.

I was just beginning to recover when I felt her hand tugging at the tear in my trousers. She cleaned my thigh wound. I was lucky that the bullet had just grazed my thigh, even so, it had hurt like hell. An inch or two to the right and I would have been in big trouble. I closed my eyes as I saw her lowering the little brown bottle of poison to repeat the process. Even though I was prepared for the pain this time, it still took my breath away.

The last thing she had brought with her was an old blanket. I told her I wanted to lie on it to make myself more comfortable rather than use it as a cover. It was far too hot for me to need anything over me at night. She began to clear the area around where I was lying, moving aside fragments of stone and splinters of wood. When she was satisfied that there was nothing left that would make me uncomfortable, she lay the blanket down beside me.

It took a while, but eventually with her help I managed to move across. The effort left me exhausted. I lay still to recover and listened to her talking. I must have drifted off to sleep. When I awoke Julia had gone. She had left the little bowl of lentils and the bottle of water. I wondered if she would come again. I felt a little stronger, that was for sure, but I wasn't ready to move anywhere yet.

It was good that I was starting to think in a more positive fashion now, and that was entirely thanks to the girl – without her I would surely have died. Now, I was beginning to wonder what I should do when I was able to get up off the floor. Should I try to walk along the road to Corbera de Ebro? How far away was it? I might not be able to walk for too long with my wounded thigh. What if I got there and the Brigade had moved on to Gandesa? There was also the possibility that we had been defeated at Corbera and been chased back through the hills to the river. One thing that I knew for sure was that I was alone, no one was going to come looking for me or anything.

If I was found wandering around on my own I risked being shot as a deserter, although hopefully if I was walking towards the front rather than heading for the rear it would be obvious that I was trying to rejoin my unit and not running away. I must confess though that I was worried about what the Commissar might make of my having disappeared for several days.

I lay perfectly still through the long heat of the afternoon, keeping my breathing shallow, resting my bruised body and willing it to get strong again. The cicadas kept me company as I drifted in and out of sleep.

When the day at last began to show some signs of cooling, I eased myself up into a sitting position against the wall. I had to close my eyes for a while to overcome a terrible dizziness that made me feel nauseous, but when my head finally cleared it felt like a big achievement. I ate a little bit more of the lentils the girl had left and drank a mouthful of her water. And there I sat, watching the dust drift aimlessly around the room as the sun slowly faded. I wasn't looking forward to darkness when the scurrying of rodents would begin. I thought I might try to stay awake all night.

*

I awoke in the morning, still sitting upright against the wall. My body was stiff as anything, but my head hurt just a bit less than the previous day. I found myself thinking about the girl, wondering if she would come back. I wanted to tell her I was feeling a bit stronger, and that it was all thanks to her. I sipped at the water she had left, glad that I could raise the bottle for myself. If she didn't come, what then? I was still too weak to walk around, and without the food that she brought I could still waste away and die in this little ruined house.

I thought about my war, I thought about Billy's war. Poor Billy from the docks in London. And I thought about my brother Stephen. Maybe he was alive. What would happen if he made it back to England only to be told that his younger brother had gone to the war to find him and that he had gone missing? I imagined my poor mother, alone in our house, grieving for the loss of her two sons. Had she already been told that I was missing? How long did these things take? I knew she had been determined to hold out hope that my brother wasn't dead, would she do the same for me? What, if by some miracle, I survived and he didn't, would she ever forgive me?

I spent a frustrating morning searching for any sound that might indicate Julia's approach, but none came. There was nothing out of the ordinary. Even the war had gone silent. The sound of the guns had disappeared which I took to be a good sign, it meant that we had captured our original objectives and advanced further into Nationalist territory. Maybe the Russian Commissar had been right, perhaps this was the great battle to turn the war in our favour. A Republican victory against all odds at this stage of the war might help to persuade the British and French that the legitimate government of Spain was not a lost cause after all.

When the heat of midday began to boil in through the broken hole in the wall of my house, I gave up waiting for her and eased myself down onto the blanket, curled myself up as best I could, and resolved to slumber my way through to evening. I was careful to avoid lying on my wounded thigh, and rested my head on my arm as a pillow. I don't know what ointment the girl had put on my wounds, but it had certainly started the healing process. Maybe it was just the passing of time that had numbed the pain, or the fact that I had had something to eat that had made me feel stronger, I don't know.

I had to decide what I was going to do if Julia didn't return. I guess I had two options. The first was to stay curled up on the blanket she had given me and slowly fade away like a dying animal. The second was to drag myself off my death bed and hope to find something vaguely edible that groups of soldiers from two different armies, Julia when she had gone looking around her family's venta and an army of rats and mice had not yet discovered. Neither option sounded particularly promising.

There was water somewhere, even if Juila had only found a bucketful, but maybe the venta had a well in its garden. I could fill my water bottle and Julia's glass bottle and head up into the hills and hope to live off the land or something. But I was a city boy and I didn't even have my rifle to hunt with, what chance did I have of living as a solo guerrilla? None at all.

If I was caught by my own side I would be shot as a deserter and if I was caught by the Fascists I would be shot as a foreign spy. If I tried to steal a chicken from an isolated farm I might get shot by an angry farmer. If I found the front and rejoined my unit then I might get shot at again in battle. If I went back to the River Ebro and crossed over to our side I would be shot by the Commissar who was, in my imagination, still striding the bank waiting for cowards and deserters. There was certainly a lot of shooting going on in my imagination at that moment. Maybe I was starting to lose my mind.

I was still hungry. Give your stomach nothing but watery soup for several weeks and it gets used to it, but treat it to something more substantial like lentils and it starts going crazy for more. My stomach was crying out to be fed, almost as loud and as annoying as the ever-bleating cicadas.

*

Julia came late afternoon, long after I had given up hope that she was going to show. She bustled in quickly through the wrecked door and tried to push it upright behind her into its proper place but without much success.

"Hi," she said almost in a whisper.

"What's wrong?" I asked her.

"I was on the way here this morning but I was being followed, so I turned around and went home. I don't think I've been followed now, but I'm not sure."

"Who's following you?" I wanted to know, if it was the Fascists out looking for Republican stragglers then I was in big trouble.

"It was Alfonso, my aunt's neighbour's son. He's got a crippled leg. He thinks we're going to be married some day. He often used to come to the venta and just sit and watch me for hours. He gives me the creeps."

"Do you think he'd give me away?"

"I don't know. Someone told the Fascists that my uncle was a Republican, it could have been Alfonso. His father has always wanted to get his hands on their land."

"I hope he didn't see you coming here."

"It's all right. I kept looking back behind me and I didn't see him. It's obvious most times when he follows me. I just start running and he can't keep up."

"Did you bring any food?" I asked unable to resist any longer.

"Of course, sorry, you must be starving."

"I need to get my strength back."

"Yes, and then where will you go? Back to the front to get shot again? You might not be so lucky next time."

"I don't know, I haven't decided yet. It's going to be a few more days before I'm strong enough to walk anywhere."

She looked into my eyes for a long time as if she was trying to read my mind, and I looked back. Her eyes, which were the darkest brown I had ever seen, seemed to draw my thoughts out of my head. Eventually, she snapped out of her trance-like state and remembered that I wanted food. From her basket she took out a parcel of food wrapped up in a cloth. She opened it and gave me a small piece of chorizo and a chunk of bread. It wasn't army bread either, it was home-made bread that didn't taste of sawdust and sand and was thick with the seeds and husks it contained. I devoured most of it as she looked on in amazement. She had never seen a starving man eat before - it can't have been a pretty sight.

With great willpower, I somehow managed to stop myself from eating it all in one go. I remembered that it was good to keep something back for the next meal in case nothing else presented itself. I put the half-eaten piece of bread and the last bite of chorizo back onto the cloth they had been wrapped up in.

"Do you want some?" I asked the girl thinking that maybe this was her daily allowance that she was saving up for me. I didn't want her starving herself.

"It's all right, we've still got more than enough food at the farm. The soldiers didn't take much when they arrested my uncle, just a few chickens and some potatoes. My aunt made my cousin hide a lot of their supplies in the hills after that."

"Sounds like a good idea. What about you and your parents? The venta was ransacked, wasn't it?"

"There's only my dad and me. My mother died a long time ago now. I guess we'll stay at the farm for the winter. Maybe we'll come home in the spring if the war comes to an end."

"I expect it will be over soon. This attack was a bit of a forlorn hope."

"So why do people keep fighting? I just want things to go back to how they were before."

"Things will never be the same again," I told her.

"I guess not. I just hope we can reopen the venta one day."

"What's the venta called?"

"Didn't you see the name painted on the wall? It's in big red letters, how did you miss it?"

"I was being shot at, remember?"

"Of course. It's called the Venta El Angel. When my father first saw my mother he thought she was an angel come down from heaven so he changed the name of his tavern in her honour."

"That's a nice story," I said. I looked at the girl's face and wondered if she looked like her mother. It was easy to believe that someone might think that she too was an angel, especially a wounded young soldier who had stared death in the face a long way from home.

CHAPTER SIX

I spent the night sitting upright with my back against the wall. Having slept through most of the afternoon, I wasn't that tired. Instead, I listened in torment to the sounds around me. Added to the dreaded rummaging of rodents and the slithering of snakes were the imagined sounds of Fascists searching through the neighbouring buildings looking for me. The wind got up in the early hours of the morning to bang half-broken shutters and whistle through the holes in the walls and roofs. It sounded like demons come to tear me apart. Even the cicadas had gone quiet. Perhaps the wind had blown them all away.

I had thought to save my remaining bread and chorizo for breakfast, but just before dawn, when the wind was threatening to tear the roof off my house, I decided to eat to take my mind off things. Then, if I did somehow fall asleep, it wouldn't be stolen by the rats. Since taking the last of my army bread however they hadn't got too close again. Maybe they had found it inedible.

I awoke with a start as something clattered on the roof above me. It scared me half to death, but in the end I concluded that it was only a loose tile that had finally given way. It was early morning and the first weak fingers of light were beginning to creep in through the hole in the wall. It was the beginning of another day. I was convinced that I was feeling stronger. If the girl came I could ask her to help me to stand upright. I wondered how soon I might be able to walk without feeling dizzy. I was no doctor, of course, but I thought I had probably been suffering from the effects of concussion after my blow to the head, that would explain my constant drowsiness and the terrible throbbing pain inside my skull like a thousand hammers trying to hammer their way out.

My little house was beginning to make me feel claustrophobic. I longed to get up and walk about, to feel the sun on my face again, even though it had tormented me so much since I had been in Spain. Spain, did I really want to die for Spain? That wasn't why I had come, and now I knew that I wasn't going to find my brother. No one knew where anyone was. He might possibly be alive, held in some prison either by our side or theirs. He might have deserted and be living wild somewhere, he was certainly more adaptable than I was. But more than likely he was dead, his body rotting forgotten in a ditch.

I think that was the moment I gave up on the war in Spain, the moment when I accepted that my brother was dead. All I wanted to do now was to get home. But home was so very far away.

The girl came soon afterwards, pushing quickly in through the broken door. She said she had come to have breakfast with me and she produced a freshly-baked loaf of bread and broke it in two. It was still warm and smelt wonderful. She smiled at me as she ate, taking small bites and chewing thoughtfully. I tried not to rush, to make each mouthful last longer, but it was difficult. My instinct was to cram it all into my mouth and swallow it almost without chewing, the quicker it got to my stomach the better. My mother would have been scandalised that I no longer ate in a civilised fashion.

After we had eaten the bread and drunk some fresh water, the girl set about cleaning my wounds again. She was so gentle that it almost didn't hurt this time. When she had finished cleaning my forehead, she surprised me by slowly letting her fingers trail down the side of my face. I could hear them scraping over the short hairs of the beard I must be growing. I hadn't shaved since we left the barracks to march to the front. I realised that I hadn't washed either. My hair was filthy and matted with blood, and my uniform was in a terrible state. Of course my spare clothes were in my kitbag which I had had to leave behind.

"Is there a well at the venta?" I asked the girl.

"Yes, of course," she replied.

"I'd like to have a wash," I decided.

"Shall I bring you a bucket of water?"

"No, I want to go there. I need to get out of this place or I'm going to go mad."

She laughed.

"Do you think you can walk?"

"There's only one way to find out." She tried to help me to stand up, but as soon as I went to put any weight on my right leg a sharp jolt of pain shot through me. It was so sudden and so acute that I almost passed out. I collapsed back onto the floor with a disappointed groan.

"It's too soon," she whispered. "You'll just have to be more patient."

I sat there gasping for breath as if I had run a marathon or something. I looked at the wound on my thigh and noticed that it had started to bleed. The girl saw it too.

"Can you bring me that bucket of water?" I asked her.

"Sure," she said and she disappeared out of the house towards the venta. I just sat there defeated, drawing in air to my lungs as fast as I could, panting like a dog. I hated for her to see me this way.

When she returned she set the metal bucket down next to me. I dipped my fingers into the water and found it beautifully cool. I splashed a bit up to my face and had to close my eyes at the luxurious feeling it gave me. Then I leant over the bucket and splashed a couple of good handfuls upwards and reached round and rubbed the back of my neck. I must have been filthy. Filthy from the dust of the tracks we had walked along, filthy from the dust of the house and the dust of the explosion that had ripped out part of the wall. There was still dust floating about, you could see it meandering in the sunlight that streamed in from outside.

I decided I wanted to tip the bucket of water over my head. I told the girl and she helped me move away from the blanket so that I didn't soak it. I started to unbutton my shirt. My shirt was filthy too of course.

"I should bring a clean one," said Julia.

"No, I don't think that's a good idea. If I'm found out of uniform they'll think I was trying to desert."

"Oh, all right then. Let me at least give it a bit of a wash for you. I'll take it over to the venta, there might be a little bit of soap somewhere."

She helped me to take my shirt off. It didn't really feel like it was made of cloth any more, but some brittle almost cardboard-like material instead. When she was gone I set about washing my upper body, careful not to get my trousers wet. I noticed that my lower arms were baked brown but that my upper arms were the same pasty white they had always been. When I had finished, my whole upper body tingling with delight, I leant over to one side and poured the remaining water over my head from back to front.

It felt so good to sit there for a few seconds unable to see with the water cascading down through my hair. I let out a sigh of contentment. It was amazing what effect some basic hygiene could have on the soul. I longed for a full bath, to relax in a tub of warm water, maybe for several hours until I had washed the dirt of Spain and the smell of blood from my body and from my mind.

The girl returned with my shirt and looked around for somewhere to spread it out to dry. In the end she found an old wooden chair in a little side room and hung the shirt over the back. It slowly began to drip onto the floor. She placed the chair near the hole in the wall so that it was in the sun. Then she came to help me move back over to my blanket. I sat with my back against the rough stone wall and Julia sat beside me. I was conscious of the fact that I had no shirt on and that no girl had ever seen me in such a state of undress before, but she didn't seem disturbed by it, so I just tried to carry on as normal.

We talked for a while, always in hushed voices in case we might give ourselves away. She asked me about my home in England and I told her about our little house on the edge of the great city of London, but of course London was a world away from this little collection of rough stone hovels which was all she had ever known. I asked her if she had ever been to a city, but she seemed confused by the question. Why would she want to go to the city? Why indeed.

I could picture the life that this girl would have had if there hadn't been a war. She would marry someone local, someone like that crippled boy who followed her around, what was his name? Alfonso, yes that was it. Someone like him who would inherit a small farm up in the hills. She would be expected to have children, lots of children to help out on the farm. But now nothing was certain. A lot of the young men around had been killed in the war which had raged through this area once already, and now it was back to finish off those that might have survived the first time. If the Nationalists fought back and threw our side back across the Ebro then the war would come back again to this area. The Republic was desperate to reunite its two remaining zones, and this region was the key.

If I somehow managed to rejoin my unit, how long would I be expected to stay in Spain? I had come as a volunteer, but I guessed that one just couldn't volunteer to go home. How much longer might the war last? If this attack across the Ebro was successful then the Republic might look for further gains of Nationalist territory, especially around besieged

Madrid for example. I might be stuck here in this war for years, maybe the only way out was in a coffin.

I leant my head back against the wall and closed my eyes, the girl moved closer and rested her head against my chest. She talked on quietly for a while but eventually stopped. From the regular pattern of her breathing I guessed that she had dozed off and then I must have fallen asleep too. She awoke with a start at about midday, gathered her things in a hurry and told me that she had to get back she had stayed far too long. If her father started to get suspicious he might make her stay in the house. He thought she was doing work on the farm to help her aunt, not playing nurse to a wounded foreign soldier.

As she reached the door I asked her when she was going to come back. Soon was all she said and with a little wave she was gone. I was left with the feeling of her head still upon my chest and the smell of her hair in the air all around me.

*

The hours were beginning to pile up upon me. Apart from the time I spent in Julia's company, my little ruined house was beginning to feel like a prison. I knew every whitewashed stone of every wall by heart. I knew the shape of the hole that had been blown open so well I could see it when I closed my eyes. The damp patches on the ceiling I had converted into distinct shapes and invented stories around them. I was even starting to distinguish the different chattering voices of the cicadas. Soon I would be giving them names and talking back to them. Of course I spent hours thinking about home, back to that idyllic place where I had grown up a step behind my brother, wearing his cast off clothes and already worn out shoes. I had hated that, I had hated seeing him given something new to wear knowing that whatever he discarded would be forced upon me.

There had never been much money. My erstwhile father, famous war hero and poet, didn't remember us very often. He always forgot our birthdays and rarely provided something for Christmas. But I don't recall my mother complaining. She made do with his infrequent monetary offerings and earned what she could by sewing for her neighbours. She was an excellent seamstress, and as a small child I would sit in the gloom of our front room watching the flash of her scissors and needles. I think that was when I felt closest to her, watching her at her work, listening to her singing softly to herself the old songs from her distant past.

How I longed to be back there now in that cramped little house. How I longed to wake up in my own bed in the early hours of a winter morning, my teeth chattering with the cold, blowing my freezing breath out as if it were smoke, and the sound of my brother's soft snoring from the other bed. My mother would be moving about in the kitchen below, grumbling about the cold that she could never get used to, as she struggled to light the fire. The fire was her daily battle and she didn't always win. Sometimes we would come down for breakfast to find the kitchen a frozen hell and my mother sitting silently sobbing on a chair, her hair deranged and her mind off somewhere else as she rocked herself gently to and fro. On those mornings we grabbed whatever we could find and hurried off to school before she came to her senses and attacked the fire once more for our benefit.

My brother and I rolled up fire lighters every night before we went to bed, as many as we could from the newspapers we had managed to scrounge from our neighbours, but often we just couldn't provide enough for our mother to get the job done. It was a great relief to her every summer when she could forget about heating the house. I'm sure there must have been a thousand times when she cursed ever having left her home on the island of Menorca, but she never said anything to us.

CHAPTER SEVEN

The girl came back in the middle of the afternoon when the day was at its hottest, far sooner than I had expected her. She said that her father had fallen asleep from exhaustion after helping on the farm all morning. He wasn't used to carrying out physical tasks. His working life had been spent in the venta's tiny kitchen preparing the day's stew, which he would then spend the lunch hour slopping onto cracked plates for his daughter to serve to the sparsely populated tables of the dining room.

Julia told me that the little venta had never been busy, being stuck as it was on a little crossroads where two minor roads met as they skirted around the hills, but that before the war they had somehow managed to survive. All the ingredients they used came from the family farm not too far away which her father's brother had worked until his execution at the hands of the Fascists. Julia said her young cousin was doing his best to help out, but he was just a child. She thought that maybe her father would decide that they should stay on at the farm rather than reopen the venta.

"What will you do after the war?" she asked me.

"I wanted to go to university. Don't expect I'll get the chance now."

"University? To study what?"

"English Literature," I told her.

"I can read and write," she said proudly. "My father taught me, he said it's important."

"It is. You don't want to serve tables all your life, do you?"

"What's wrong with that?" she said sounding annoyed that perhaps I was making fun of her.

"If you like, when I get home, I could write you a letter," I said quickly changing the subject.

"I've never received a letter," she said.

"And you'd have to write back."

"Of course. I'd like that." And then a funny thing happened. We were sitting so close and all of a sudden our heads turned towards each other at the same moment and I leaned forward and kissed her. I don't know what made me do it. I'd never kissed a girl before, I'd never even wanted to, but something inside me, deep inside, made me want to kiss that girl at that moment. Our lips touched just briefly before she jumped to her feet and raced away, half stumbling over a broken table that blocked her path to the door.

"I'm sorry," I called out after her, but she didn't pause in her flight. I had upset her and I cursed myself for being such an idiot. Perhaps she would tell her father and he would come and shoot me, or perhaps she would tell Alfonso her crippled neighbour and he would send the Fascists to get me as soon as our army had been beaten back. Or, worse still, she would just never come to see me again. I held my head in my hands for a long time and tried desperately not to cry at my stupidity.

It was a while later that I saw she had left her little basket behind. I looked inside and found some goat's milk cheese wrapped in a piece of cloth and a piece of bread. There was fresh water in the bottle too, as always. And there was a pair of trousers. They were old and well-worn. They had probably belonged to her uncle. I decided to put them on, anything was better than my torn and bloodstained ones.

I must have looked a fearful sight struggling to remove my army trousers, desperately trying not to make my thigh bleed again, slithering on my blanket from side to side like a wounded snake. When I got them down around my ankles I realised that I couldn't get them off over my boots, and I lay still, defeated for a while. It was at that moment that Julia decided to come back. I heard footsteps approaching the door and I remember thinking that it was a god-awful moment to be taken by the Fascists.

She burst in through the door as if she had been running.

"I'm sorry Martin. I didn't mean to run away like that…" her voice trailed off as she saw me lying there with my trousers down around my ankles. Her face told me that she was going to turn around and run away again.

"Julia, wait. I can't get my boots off. Help me, please." I begged. She paused. In the end she decided to help me and came over and sat on the floor and started to undo the laces of my boots. She gently removed the right one first and then the left and then she stood up and walked away to the other side of the room and turned her back. I struggled to get the new trousers on as quickly as I could. They were a little too big around the waist and too short in the leg, but that was fine. I sat up against the wall, tired from my efforts.

"You can turn around now," I told her. She carefully turned around to look at me and seeing that I was respectable again she smiled and came over towards me. "I'm sorry about earlier," I told her, "it never should have happened." I was going to promise her that it would never happen again when she touched her finger to my lips to make me stop talking.

"It's all right," she whispered. "You just surprised me, that's all. No one's ever kissed me before." She slowly removed her finger from my lips and we sat there looking into each other's eyes. Then she leaned forward and we kissed again, longer this time. I felt my heart pounding in my chest like it was going to burst or something. Then she broke away, gave me one of her beautiful smiles and set about putting my boots back on. I noticed there was a bright red stain starting to appear on my new trousers and I put my hand down over it. When my boots were retied, she picked my army trousers up off the floor and went over to the venta to wash them.

*

The next day in the early afternoon, she brought a needle and thread and I sat and watched as she darned the hole in my trousers. She said I had been very lucky, but I knew that. I knew that if either of my wounds had been just slightly more serious then I would have died, and I also knew that without her help I would have died too.

I looked at her face rapt in concentration as she worked, her tongue protruding slightly between her lips. I watched the gentle rise and fall of her chest and imagined I could hear her heartbeat. It was strange to think that there was still a terrible civil war going on, and that in the short time it took her to mend a tear in a pair of trousers maybe several hundred men and women had been killed. I watched as she tied off her needlework and bit off the remaining thread.

I was snapped suddenly back to reality by the sound of someone trying to open the door of the house. I saw a look of panic cross the girl's face and she sprang to her feet and ran across the room. She arrived just as a small boy emerged from behind the door.

"Primo!" she shouted at him. "What're you doing here?"

"Wanted to see if the soldier was dead yet," he shouted back at her.

"You shouldn't be here."

"Neither should you, Prima. I'm going to tell your father." The boy gave me a quick look just to make sure that I was indeed still alive and then turned to leave.

"Wait, Miguelito," said Julia grabbing at his arm to stop him from leaving. "I'm sorry I shouted, you mustn't tell my father, you hear?"

"Why? Is he a Fascist?"

"No, he's one of ours."

"Doesn't look like one of ours."

"He's not from here, but he's on our side."

"And what are you doing here?"

"I'm helping him to get better. I bring him a little food each day so that he gets stronger."

"Does my mother know you're stealing food?"

"It's not stealing, it's helping someone. Didn't the Priest tell us every Sunday to help those who can't help themselves?"

"I guess so. But they shot him."

"Yes, but he was a good man, wasn't he?"

The boy nodded slowly. He looked at me again. I gave him a smile to try to make him see that I wasn't dangerous and that I wouldn't do him any harm, or his cousin for that matter.

"I want to go home," decided the boy.

"Sure," agreed Julia, "I'll go with you, you shouldn't be roaming around on your own."

She came over to me and collected her things.

"It's all right," she whispered, "he won't tell." She threw me my trousers which she had dropped on the floor when her cousin had arrived.

I listened to them go until I couldn't hear their voices any more. The sensible thing to do would be to leave. Her cousin might not let himself be persuaded that he should keep the secret. I didn't want to be sitting around waiting for the Fascists or perhaps worse still Julia's father.

The first thing to do was to get back into my army trousers. I really didn't want to be out of uniform if soldiers of either side ended up coming for me. I'd heard that the Rebels shot captured Brigadistas as spies and that if I had the misfortune to meet members of the Moroccan army then it was better to kill myself than to be taken alive. Apparently they did unspeakable things to their prisoners. I was only slightly less worried that my own side would treat me as a deserter.

The best thing to do would be to somehow rejoin my unit and hope that my Captain would take care of me. I could still be valuable to him if he hadn't found a new liaison officer. I wondered if he had written a letter to my mother, did they do that in this war? Would he say that I had died bravely attacking an enemy position and that I was a credit to my unit? Probably he wouldn't have written yet as I would still be listed as missing. Perhaps he thought I had run away. That made me all the more determined to rejoin my unit. I didn't want my father to be told that I had been a coward.

I struggled to change back into my army trousers for well over an hour. If Julia's Primo had told her father then I was running out of time. But I was exhausted. I sat breathing deeply for a while, my senses on edge for any approaching enemy. When I felt rested enough, I inched my way up the wall until I was just about standing. I instantly felt light headed and if I hadn't been clutching at a protruding stone I would have fallen straight away. I stood as still as I could and willed myself not to collapse.

After a few minutes, I convinced myself that it was all right to move again. I edged just slightly along the wall to my left, towards the gaping hole that was the nearest exit. When I reached it, my eyes were temporarily blinded by the sudden brightness of the sun. I felt dizzy and out of breath. Eventually, I went outside for the first time in what seemed like forever.

The first thing I saw was the blood on the dirt of the road where Billy and I had been shot. Billy's body had been taken away and my rifle was gone also. I had sort of hoped that my rifle might still be there. I knew that my having lost it might make me seem even more like a deserter, and also I would have liked to have had it in case the dreaded Moors found me. To be able to shoot myself if need be rather than to make some sort of heroic last stand. And what about the girl? If she was caught with me she would be shot also, either for hiding a deserter or for helping an enemy spy. She was risking her life and I knew I wasn't worth it.

That decided me, I would have to leave this place and put as much distance as I could between myself and the girl, for her sake. There was nothing I would have liked more at that time than to have forgotten about the war and stayed there with her indefinitely. Maybe I could help her reopen the venta and do the washing up or something. I couldn't cook and I would probably drop all the plates if I tried to wait tables, but I reckoned I could handle the washing up. And I wouldn't want any wages. I could sleep in a cupboard or something and eat the leftovers from mealtimes. It would be enough for me just to be able to spend time with Julia.

My first thought was to cross the road to the venta and fill my water bottle from the well in the garden there. I didn't even make it half way across the road before I felt as if I had run a marathon. I began to feel sick in my stomach, but I gathered up all the determination I could muster and stumbled on until I reached the low stone wall on the opposite side of the road. I had to sit down to get my breath back. I felt terribly exposed out there, and I spent the whole time looking in every direction to see if anyone was coming. Fortunately, there was no one around. Only soldiers or fools would venture out in the middle of a war. I of course was both.

When my breathing returned to normal, I stumbled alongside the wall until I came to the door to the venta. I saw the lock was broken so I pushed my way inside. I found a little dining room with its wooden chairs and tables still in place, as if waiting for the evening dinner service. There was a wooden-topped counter on the far side which must have been the bar area, but no bottles remained, just a few broken glasses and an earthenware jug. There was a door that led through to the cramped little kitchen and at the end of the room a set of double doors that must lead out to the garden.

I found the locks on the double doors had been broken also. Outside, in the middle of the courtyard, was the well. There was a large untamed lemon tree too, but no ripe fruit, just hundreds of small green balls of would-be lemons. I guess those who had been there before me had taken anything that was even remotely edible from the venta including the lemons from its tree.

I sat on the stone rim of the well and looked down. I could just make out the dark water at the bottom. The metal bucket that the girl had brought over for me to wash from was tied to the end of a rope that went up through a pulley suspended out above the well. I lowered the bucket, dipped it below the surface of the water and then hauled it up.

I filled my army water bottle and then drank my fill from the bucket using cupped hands before washing my sweaty face and neck. When I looked up at the sky I realised that it was late afternoon already and that there wouldn't be too much daylight left. I decided to wait until the morning before setting off up the road towards Corbera de Ebro. I went and sat under the lemon tree to rest before looking for somewhere to spend the night. There was a stone flight of steps that led up the side of the building to the first floor where I guessed the bedrooms were. I could sleep on the girl's bed if the soldiers hadn't stolen her mattress. It would be a luxury after so many nights spent sleeping on a hard stone floor.

CHAPTER EIGHT

I was awoken the next morning, by someone shouting my name. It came into a dream so slowly that for a long time I wasn't sure if it was real or not. But it was repeated again and again, each time a little closer. Gradually I realised that it was the girl's voice. She had come looking for me in the house where I had always been. I had meant to wake up early and try to walk towards the front, wherever that might be, but she was here already, before I'd had the chance to set off.

I heard her enter the venta and call out my name once more, it sounded so forlorn and desperate that it pulled at my heart strings.

"I'm up here," I called out to her. She was going to find me anyway, so I didn't want to make her suffer any more than she already had.

I heard her burst out through the doors into the garden and run up the stairs to the first floor. Out of breath she reached the doorway to her room where I was lying on her lumpy straw-filled mattress on the floor in the corner.

"Martin, I thought they'd taken you," she gasped and then she rushed over to me and grabbed me into her arms, pressing her face against my neck. I felt her boiling tears against my skin as she started to cry, great heaving sobs that racked her whole body. It was a while before she pulled herself away and when she did she looked into my eyes as was her habit.

"Thought I'd sleep somewhere more comfortable," I told her.

"Why didn't you tell me yesterday?"

"Only thought of it last night."

"I thought you were gone."

"I was going to go back to the house and wait for you when I woke up. I just slept a little too long that's all."

"Don't do that again," she said. Her eyes were still full of tears, but I think they were tears of relief. I don't think she thought I was lying to her. She leaned in and kissed me on the mouth and then she lay down beside me on the mattress and rested her head on my chest. I stroked her hair. She began to calm down.

After a while, she sat up beside me. I saw she was looking at my ammunition pouch, which I had brought with me and my army water bottle.

"You were going to leave, weren't you?"

"Listen Julia, I'm scared that if anyone finds me here that something terrible might happen to you. Helping a deserter or an enemy soldier, well, you could be shot. Surely you know that."

"I don't care," was all she said and she kissed me again. "I don't want you to leave."

"But I can't stay here forever."

"Why not?"

"Because I'm a soldier and there's a war and it's impossible."

"If you go then I'm going with you. There are women fighting aren't there?"

"Yes, but I don't want you to fight."

"Why not?"

"Because I don't want anything bad to happen to you."

"Now you know how I feel," she said triumphantly. I was about to continue with the conversation when she put her finger against my lips.

"Let's have breakfast," she said. "I can't stay too long I've got work to do at the farm."

*

In the late afternoon, she came back and we curled up together on her mattress and I promised her that I wouldn't go away, that I would stay with her forever. She seemed happy about this and lay beside me, smiling, whilst I stroked her beautiful long hair. And so it was decided, I was a deserter. Looking back it was the worst possible decision I could have taken, but at the time it was an easy one to make. I naively thought that somehow I could remain hidden away until the war came to an end, that the victorious rebels would pardon those who had fought against them, and that Julia's father would welcome me into the family and let me stay.

It's quite possible that Julia had just saved my life for a second time. Had I set off towards the front in my weakened state I might well have collapsed at the roadside from exhaustion and died. Maybe that would have been the best thing that could have happened, especially for poor Julia.

As the sun began to fade away, the girl decided that she had to go. I hated it when she left. I hated being without her. I stumbled down the stone steps behind her to the little garden and we kissed goodbye. Afterwards, I sat on the wall of the well, in the long shadow of the lemon tree and waited for it to get dark. I was alone, but I was happy, I was in her house and I felt her presence all around me.

When it was dark, I hobbled across to my former dwelling to get the blanket which I took back to Julia's little bedroom at the venta. Her father's room had had a hole blown open in the roof, but I wouldn't have wanted to stay there anyway.

When Julia didn't come for breakfast the next morning, I went to her father's bedroom and inspected the large wardrobe there. Anything decent he would have taken with him when they left, but there was an old pair of trousers and a couple of wrinkled shirts hanging up. I found a threadbare sweater and decided to borrow it for when the nights started to get colder and to use as a pillow in the meantime. It was early August and the summer was still ablaze, but I had no uniform for autumn or winter. We had only been given very basic kit for a summer campaign. I suppose that those who were still alive at the end of the summer would be issued with warmer clothes to keep them fighting through the colder months, if of course the Republic survived until winter. It was now in my interests that the Republicans lost the war as soon as possible and of course I felt like a terrible traitor.

I continued to explore the little venta. I found the entrance to the cellar at the side of the house and went down to have a look. It took a long while for my eyes to grow accustomed to the gloom, but when they did I was able to explore. They must have kept supplies down there once, but everything had been looted by starving soldiers. There were a few empty flour sacks and some small wooden crates that would have been used to bring fruit and vegetables from the farm.

There was a low wall that ran down near the far side which might have been some sort of animal enclosure for the worst months of winter, but I wasn't sure. I thought it might make a good place to hide if any soldiers came looking for me. It would be safer than Julia's bedroom that was for sure. In the gloom of the cellar, lying hidden down behind the wall I might just go unnoticed. I figured that most soldiers wouldn't spend long down in a cellar once they realised that there was nothing edible there.

I stumbled across a small metal bathtub and remembered how long it was since I had known the luxury of a real bath. I decided to take it up to the garden and fill it with water. It took a lot of effort to haul it up the steep stairs from the cellar, but I figured it would be worth it. I set it down in the full sun beside the well and sat for a while to get my breath back. Then I began to haul up bucketfuls of water.

I had planned to leave it for a few hours so that the sun would heat up the water a bit, but when it was about half full I couldn't resist any longer. I quickly stripped off my clothes and stepped into the tub. The water was cold, but my need to feel clean was greater and I sat down quickly and let the water cover me. The tub was so small that I had to sit with my knees up, but that didn't matter. I rested my head back against the metal and closed my eyes resisting the temptation to start shivering uncontrollably.

After a while, my body adapted to the temperature of the water and I no longer felt so cold. I was just about to close my eyes and have a long rest when I heard someone opening the door of the venta. My first thought was to leap out of the bathtub, but I had no towel, so in the end I decided to stay put. It was almost certainly Julia. I heard her muffled footsteps cross the stone floor of the dining room, and then she came out into the garden. She gasped when she saw me sitting in the bathtub, and then she laughed.

"Look at you," she giggled, "you're too big for it."

I smiled dumbly at her, wondering how long I was going to have to stay in the tub. I had planned to simply sit in the sun to get dry, but I couldn't do that now she was here.

"I don't suppose you know where the soap is?" I asked her.

"I found some in the kitchen when I washed your shirt, I'll go get it."

When she came back she handed me a small piece of white soap. I pulled some water up over my head and tried to work up some lather with the soap. I heard her laughing.

"Here, let me do it," she said and she came over and took the piece of soap from my hand. Within no time my hair was full of foam, although she was careful not to touch my scalp wound. I sat very still with my hands in my lap. Soon she began the job of rinsing. When she finished with my hair she cleaned my face and neck and then went down to my shoulders. I closed my eyes and let her work. Her touch was like electricity sparking all across my upper body.

"You'll have to stand up if you want me to do the rest," she stated matter-of-factly.

"I'm naked," I stuttered.

"I know."

Keeping my eyes firmly closed I tried to stand up in the tub without using my hands, but it was impossible. In the end, I just gave up and pushed on the sides of the tub until I was standing. I quickly dropped my hands to cover myself, but if she had been looking then she must have seen me.

"You can open your eyes you know," she giggled. I thought perhaps she was enjoying my distress. I looked at her and she was smiling. She stepped back towards me and began to work on my chest. When her hand reached as low as my stomach it was as if a cramp shot across from one side to the other. Then she did it again, and the cramp came again. It almost made me feel nauseous but I didn't ask her to stop.

She walked around behind me and soaped my back, running her slippery fingers across my shoulder blades and up and down my spine. I'd never spent more than a couple of minutes in a bath before, especially since I had always had to use my brother's dirty water, but this girl seemed determined to leave me cleaner than I had ever been in my life.

"Sit down and I'll rinse you off," she told me quietly.

I sat back into the tub as quickly as I could and she began pouring water up and over me using her cupped hands.

"You can do the rest," she said. I quickly washed what she hadn't and handed her back the piece of soap.

"I haven't got a towel," I informed her.

"You'll just have to dry off in the sun."

"I'll wait until you leave."

"Don't be silly. Out you get. Besides, it's a pity to tip away the water after only one person."

I didn't know what she meant and seeing my enquiring look she started to unbutton her blouse. Was she really going to have a bath right there in front of me? I eased myself up out of the water and stepped out of the tub onto the flagstones of the patio. Water was dripping off me everywhere. The sun on my skin was a relief. I saw her still undoing her little buttons and I turned away to give her some privacy. I heard her get into the tub a little while later.

"The water's cold. You should have waited for the sun to heat it up a bit more," she said.

"I was impatient to get in." I told her.

"Come and wash me then," she called out. I hesitated. If I washed her I would have to use my hands and then I would have nothing to hide myself with. "Don't you want to?" she asked.

Of course I wanted to. I turned slowly and saw her sitting in the tub. She didn't look as cramped up as I had been. I went over to her. She ducked down into the water as far as she could and I scooped water up over her head. Then I picked up the soap from the floor and began to work it into her hair as she had done with mine. I took my time. She had long hair and there was a lot to cover but that suited me just fine. Eventually she was satisfied that I had done the job adequately and she let me rinse off the soap. I moved onto her face and neck and then she surprised me by standing up and turning her back so that I could wash that too.

I tried not to look at her naked body as I worked with trembling hands but it was impossible not to. Her skin was so white, almost like marble. I could see the outlines of her ribcage and the curve of the bottom of her spine. I played my hands slowly across her back as she had done to me. When I was finished I rinsed off the soap and she turned slowly to face me. She looked deep into my eyes. It unnerved me the way she did that, but I liked it too.

"Now the front," she whispered. I did her shoulders and arms and then looked at her for permission to touch her chest. She didn't say anything but gave me a slight smile. I began to caress the soap across the top of her chest and slowly, expecting her to stop me at any moment, I let my hands slide lower and lower towards her breasts. When I finally touched them I heard her gasp. I instantly pulled my hands away.

"It's all right," she whispered, "don't stop."

CHAPTER NINE

We sat together on the little wall of the well in the middle of the patio drying slowly in the sun. We started off holding hands and kissing occasionally, but what I really wanted to do was touch her breasts again, so after a while I did. She didn't stop me. She leant back slightly and turned her face up to the sun and I spent ages gently caressing her. It was like some unbelievable dream that you know won't last.

That night I couldn't sleep. I lay awake listening to the wind sneaking in through the hole in the roof of the room next door, tugging at the loose tiles and generally making mischief. I thought about Julia. The hours without her seemed like years, whilst the minutes we shared together seemed to evaporate in seconds. I thought about her body, so thin you could see the outline of her ribs and her hip bones and of course it was the most beautiful thing I had ever known.

In the morning, whilst I waited for her to arrive with breakfast, I hunted around for some tools. I had decided that I was going to fix the hole that had been blown in the venta's roof. It needed to be done before the winter although there was the terrible possibility that the war might return once more and blow more holes in the place. I had never built or mended anything in my life, but I wanted to do it to show Julia's father that I could be useful.

As I went from one abandoned dwelling to the next, I studied the inside of the roofs to get an idea of what I was taking on. I would just help myself to any materials I needed from the house where I had been living before which was in a far worse state then any of the others and would probably need to be pulled down rather than patched up. I wondered what had happened to the people from the other houses. Perhaps they too had escaped into the hills to be with family members who lived there, or perhaps they had been taken away by one side or the other at some time in the war.

In the end, I found an old rusty hammer and a blunt saw. The people here had obviously been poor and of course any decent tools would have been prized possessions that they would have taken away with them when they fled. I went to Julia's father's room and studied the hole that had been blown open. The sky that I could see through it was a blue so clear that I had never known growing up in England, the light so bright that it dazzled my eyes. I couldn't think what to do first, so I decided to go down to the patio and wait for Julia. When she left I would get down to work. I didn't want her to see what I was up to I wanted to present her with the finished repair as a surprise.

I drew up some water from the well and had a drink and washed my face. I felt the roughness of my growing beard and for a long while I sat on the wall letting the gathering strength of the sun dry me off. It was mid morning when I decided that Julia hadn't been able to get away unnoticed and so I went back to inspect the hole in the roof again. If anything, this time, it looked even bigger and an even more-daunting proposition. The best time to tackle it would be in the cool of the late afternoon I decided, so I headed back to the patio and sat in the shade of the lemon tree on a chair I had brought out from the dining room. When I became drowsy with the heat and uncomfortable sitting on the chair I went to have a sleep in the room upstairs.

*

Julia didn't come that day. It was the first time since we had met that a whole day had passed without us being together. I was hungry of course, but more than that I was worried that she might not come again. I hoped that I hadn't offended her or anything.

I didn't start work on patching up the hole in the roof, but I did start to clear away the broken tiles and splintered beams from the floor. I was happy that I had at least made some sort of a start. There was no hurry. Winter was still a long way away.

At dusk, as the light began to fade, I heard an unfamiliar noise whilst I was sitting in the patio on the wall of the well. At first, I thought I was imagining it, but I listened intently for a few seconds more and realised that it was definitely the slow methodical approach of a horse, its hooves resonating as they struck the stones of the crude surface of the road. My first instinct was to dash for the cellar and hide there, but then I remembered that my things were up in Julia's room. I didn't have much, but anyone who looked in would easily realise that there was a soldier hiding in the building.

I rushed up the stairs to the first floor and keeping low so that I couldn't be seen through the broken window, I quickly threw my things onto the mattress and then rolled it up. I retreated back down the stairs my heart racing. I could no longer hear the horse's steady approach and I was close to panicking. I almost stumbled in my haste to get down, the ungainly mattress dragging down the wall as I descended.

As I reached the top of the stone steps leading down to the cellar I heard the front door of the venta being forced open. I was now wild with panic. As soon as I reached the cellar I headed for the far side where I knew there was a low wall, but my eyes were not accustomed to the dark and I couldn't see anything. I only knew I had reached the wall when I crashed into it. I heaved the mattress over and then threw myself on top of it. I lay still, very still. I tried to calm my breathing by taking long shallow breaths, willing my heart to stop pounding in case it might give me away.

I didn't hear anything for a while and I began to hope that the stranger had looked around the venta's kitchen, found nothing and left, but then I heard the door to the patio being opened and my panic went off the scale. The footsteps across the stone slabs sounded heavy, like a big man wearing boots, like a soldier perhaps or a Guardia Civil. I was almost whimpering with fright like a small defenceless dog. My breath was coming in short gulps and sweat had broken out all over my body.

I heard the stranger begin to lower the bucket into the well to fetch up some water. I hoped that whoever it was would just quench their thirst and leave. It was almost dark now with just the faintest glow of light still coming down the stairs into the cellar. As carefully as I could, I crawled beneath the mattress taking my meagre possessions into hiding with me. In the dark of the cellar maybe I would get away with it.

I lay almost suffocating beneath the mattress my ears alert for any sound. The footsteps resumed once more, and my heart stopped beating as I realised that they were heading for the steps down to the cellar.

I knew already what it was like to be shot and now I could almost hear the sudden volley of the firing squad, feel the pain of a bullet's impact into my heart. I wanted to be sick and my stomach was tying itself up into knots. I was lucky that I hadn't eaten anything. Heavy footsteps began to descend the steps down to where I was hiding. I realised I had no kind of weapon to hand. I had always thought that when I was captured it would be by a small squad of soldiers, I had never imagined that it might be just one man who came for me.

I had been afraid to carry grenades, but if I'd had one to hand at that moment I would have used it. In the confined space of the cellar I might well have been killed too, but I'm sure that wouldn't have prevented me. At the bottom of the stairs the stranger stopped. He was obviously trying to adjust his eyes to the gloom. That would have been the moment to attack had I been armed and if I had been brave enough.

After a while, and to my great relief, the stranger began to go back up the steps to the patio. When he reached the top I allowed myself to start breathing again, hurried shallow breaths like a silently panting dog.

I continued to lie as still as I could even when a few minutes later I heard the sound of horse's hooves once more. The relief was immense, but I found that I had started to shake uncontrollably. I stayed where I was in the darkness of the cellar hidden under Julia's mattress for at least an hour, maybe more. When my heartbeat had returned to more or less normal and my breathing had slowed and I no longer felt sick, I crawled on top of the mattress and lay there behind the wall awake all night in case the stranger should return.

Towards dawn I must have fallen asleep from exhaustion, but I struggled with nightmares and when daylight came I crept up the stairs to the patio to see the light of day. It was an indescribable relief. I had really believed that I would never emerge from that dark hole. I sat on the wall by the well, closed my eyes and raised my face up the sun. It was weak as it was still early, but it was just what I needed.

The stranger had left a half-filled bucket of water and I dipped my hands in and had a long drink and then a wash. I sat there until the sun got too hot and I had to seek the shade of the lemon tree. I hadn't been there long when I heard the sound of someone forcing their way into the venta. I panicked once more and flew back down the steps into the cellar. This time there were no heavy boots and as the door to the patio opened I heard Julia softly calling my name. I had never been so happy to hear someone's voice in my life and I raced up the steps and embraced her to me. Such was my emotion that we almost toppled over.

Julia pulled back from me, a bewildered look on her face. I told her about my nightmare from the previous evening of the visit of the lone horseman. When I finished she hugged me to her as tightly as I had embraced her. It had been a close escape and we both realised that we had almost lost each other.

We sat under the lemon tree and shared a small chunk of bread together and she explained that she hadn't been able to come the previous day because her aunt was getting suspicious of her long absences, and so she had spent the day working in the vegetable garden next to the house in full view of everyone. She took out some small tomatoes, still more green than red and placed them on the floor.

"I brought you these," she told me. "You must be starving."

"Thank you," I whispered, "but I don't want to eat them right now."

"What do you want then?" she asked playfully.

"You know what I want."

She smiled and started to undo the buttons of her blouse, all the time her deep brown eyes looking into mine.

*

She didn't stay long. She was worried about what her aunt would say if she was out of sight too much. When she was gone, I carried the mattress back up to her bedroom, but I left my things hidden down in the cellar under some old dusty curtains. From now on I would have to be more careful and more alert to danger.

CHAPTER TEN

After breakfast the next day, Julia produced a cut-throat razor and some shaving soap.
"You look like a wild man from the woods," she told me. I reached out for the razor but she shook her head.
"You don't think I'm going to let you shave me, do you?" I said.
"Yes. I always shave my father."
"You do?"
"He says I'm very good at it and when your hair gets longer I'll cut that too."
I relented. You couldn't argue with someone who had saved your life and who continued to keep you alive on a daily basis. So, I sat back in a chair and let her lather up my face. She shaved me with slow delicate strokes with an obviously practised hand. She was so gentle that I almost fell asleep. I certainly felt relaxed. I found myself wondering just how long this idyllic situation could last. How long would the war continue? Could I remain undetected until its end? And what then? Imagine that the war was to end tomorrow, would there be a general spirit of forgiveness? Would Franco let all those who had fought against him just return to their towns and villages and go back to their former lives? Somehow I doubted it. What of the foreigners who had come to

fight in a war that wasn't their own? Would those that couldn't or didn't want to go home ever be forgiven? I was young and very naïve, but even I knew in my heart that there was no future for me in Spain. I knew it, but I did nothing to save myself. Worst of all I did nothing to save Julia.

When she had finished shaving me, we went upstairs to lie on her mattress. She spent what seemed like hours just stroking my new face.

*

In the afternoon, I was disturbed from a light sleep by the sound of the door to the venta being opened. I listened for Julia's voice to call out that it was her, but she didn't. I quickly jumped up and crept down the stairs to the patio. I peered in through the doors and was alarmed to see a young man moving through the dining room and heading towards the kitchen. I noticed he was limping and realised that it must be the crippled boy, Alfonso, who sometimes tried to follow Julia. I wondered at first if he had come looking for me, but when I saw that he was just curiously inspecting the venta I relaxed a little.

I crept down to the cellar and hid under the dusty curtains behind the wall and waited to see what he would do. He spent a long time moving about, dragging his almost useless left leg, so that it was easy for me to follow his progress. When he got bored of the kitchen he came out to the patio and then I heard him climbing the stairs to the bedrooms. Then there was silence, a long silence that went on deep into the afternoon. In the end, my curiosity and discomfort got the better of me and I left the cellar to see whether he had gone or not. I found him lying asleep on Julia's mattress, just where I had been a couple of hours before.

I left the venta as quietly as I could and climbed the little hill to get a view down over the houses. At the top I found the twisted remains of a field gun, the one that had been firing at us when we entered the village. There was a large crater nearby and a few bits of useless army equipment and some spent cartridges from a machine gun. I lay down and crawled forward so that I had a good view of the venta but couldn't be seen.

I kept watch in case Julia should turn up, I didn't want her to bump into her neighbour unexpectedly. When it was beginning to grow dark the crippled boy at last came out of the venta. He pulled the door shut behind him and stood for a while looking up at the sky, puzzled perhaps at why it was growing dark and wondering where the afternoon had gone. I let him get a bit of a start as he shuffled off into the hills, zigzagging slowly as he dragged along his useless leg. I followed at a safe distance just in case he might suddenly turn around, but he didn't show any signs that he thought he might be being followed. I wanted to see where he lived and then I would be able to look for Julia's house. The problem was that the light was fading fast. I hoped it wasn't far as I didn't want to get lost in the darkness.

After a while, I began to smell smoke. Up ahead I saw an old stone house tucked into the side of a low hill. There was a thin wisp of smoke coming out of the chimney which meant that Alfonso's mother must be heating up the evening leftovers. The ground around was divided into terraces, some were planted with neat fruit trees, others were used for vegetables. I could hear the clucking of hens as they tried to settle down for the night.

I hid behind a boulder and watched Alfonso until he entered the house. It was seriously starting to get dark now, that pitch black darkness that suddenly descends and catches you by surprise, even though you should have known it was coming. It reminded me of the night we had crossed the Ebro. There was only a thin sliver of moon, but its light was wrapped up in a blanket of cloud. I suddenly felt alone and afraid.

In the end, I roamed around in a circle to try to find Julia's farm, but it was just too dark and I didn't want to stray too far from the way I had come. I had no blanket and no food and in the end I just curled up behind the boulder within sight of Alfonso's house. It was a long and miserable night. I don't think I slept at all. I could hear small nocturnal animals scurrying around close at hand and I was worried that my presence might attract a wolf. I was cold too. I wasn't used to sleeping outside any more. I had got accustomed to the luxury of a straw-filled mattress and the protection of a roof and thick stone walls. When the wind got up as dawn approached, it whistled through the rocks and blew dust over my face.

When it finally started to grow light, I picked myself up and headed off to search for another farm nearby. I eventually found one, small, stony-faced and alone, nestled in a gap between two ridges. I saw the same sculpted terraces, like wide steps, leading in several different directions away from the house. There were a few trees and vegetables just as there had been at Alfonso's house. I heard a cock begin to stir, winding up its voice slowly, ready for one huge cry to coincide with the breakthrough of a new day. When it came it was startling, breaking the relative silence of the night and announcing the need for people to give up the security of their beds and come out into the world once more.

I heard a pig snuffling around in its sty, awoken by the cockerel and desperately hungry, searching for something it might have forgotten to eat the previous day. Some hens emerged from a hen house and started to peck at the ground around it, clucking quietly to each other. The cock crowed again, not quite as loud as that first shrill cry, but almost. It must be impossible to sleep after he had begun. I hoped that this was Julia's house and that she might come out to feed the animals. I was fairly close by, crouching behind a tree just a little way up the hillside from the house. Sure enough, a few minutes later she came out carrying a small bucket of scraps for the animals.

She headed first for the pigsty. The pig was snorting and obviously going crazy from hunger. She tipped the bucket of slops into the sty and the snorting stopped immediately as the pig began to eat. She then went to a little shed not far from the house and returned with a cloth sack with feed for the hens. I checked that no one else was around and then left my hiding place and descended the rocky slope down to her level. She heard my approach and looked up. The look of shock on her face was a picture to behold.

"Buenos días," I whispered somewhat formally as I scrambled the last few yards to get to her.

"What are you doing here?" she hissed not sounding quite as pleased to see me as I had hoped that she would, especially given the uncomfortable night I had suffered in order to see her. She looked back over her shoulder towards the farm house to check that no one else was about. She turned back to face me, her mouth open to start a protest, but I silenced her with a kiss. She let me kiss her for just a few seconds before breaking away.

"Are you crazy?" she demanded. Her eyes were full of anger like I had never seen them before.

"Alfonso came to the venta yesterday," I told her. Her eyes changed from anger to fear. She had the most expressive eyes I had ever seen.

"Go up to the terrace at the top," she told me, "wait for me there. I'll get us something to eat." She scattered a few handfuls of corn for the hens and then headed for the house. I scrambled back up the slope to the top terrace which was home to a few twisted old pear trees and sat out of sight waiting for her. When she arrived she held out a chunk of bread to me. I took it from her and found it hard and cold, obviously from the day before or maybe even the day before that. I broke it in two and we sat down on the hard ground beneath one of the trees and sucked at the bread to try to make it soft enough to eat.

I told her about how her crippled neighbour had come to the venta and slept through the afternoon on her mattress. She was scandalised. I told her how I had followed him back to his farm and spent the night out in the open in the hope of finding where she lived.

"What if someone sees you?" she said.

"I don't plan on anyone seeing me. Just wanted to be with you, to tell you that we need to be wary of Alfonso."

"He gives me the creeps," she whispered. "If he sees us together he won't hesitate to tell someone."

"I know."

"You ought to leave," she decided. "If my father finds you hanging around here there'll be hell to pay."

"I know that, I'm not sure of how to get back to the venta that's all."

"Well, I'll go with you. I was planning to come over this morning when we finish the washing. My aunt always needs a rest afterwards and my father is teaching Miguelito to read in the mornings after he's collected the vegetables."

She told me to stay out of sight down the track that led back towards Alfonso's house and wait for her there. I kissed her on the lips much to her annoyance and hurried off, skirting around and above the house to get away. I didn't have to go far along the track to find a suitable hiding place behind a ragged bush, through which I could still see the farm.

I spent a couple of hours there, hidden away, watching daily life on a small hill farm. The girl's father, smaller and older than I had imagined him, searched carefully between the rows of runner beans. Julia and her aunt washed some clothes and a few bed sheets. It looked like hard work as they first soaked and scrubbed everything in the iron bath tub and then put it through a large mangle that must have been in the family for generations. Finally, they hung everything up to dry on ropes strung between the different buildings of the farm.

When they had finished and her father and aunt had gone back inside, Julia came down the track towards me. I sprang out of my hiding place making her gasp. I laughed at her and then caught her up in my arms and hugged her tight. She pushed me away and scolded me, since we were still in full view of the farm, then she ran off ahead. I couldn't run as fast as her as my leg was still not right, but I tried hard to keep up. Eventually, she must have decided that we were far enough away from the farm and she slowed and then stopped. She looked round at me and saw me struggling after her and walked back towards me.

She grabbed my face and kissed me hard and then pulled me off the track into the bushes and we collapsed panting to the ground clawing at each other's clothes.

CHAPTER ELEVEN

When we got back to the venta, Julia went in first just to check that Alfonso wasn't there again. She gave me the all clear and we sat out in the patio and tried to decide what we should do about the situation. I could move into one of the other houses or back to where I had been before, but I liked living at the venta, besides, I wanted to repair the roof before winter came. In the end, we decided that I should lean a chair back under the door handle of the front door to make it more difficult for someone to get inside. I placed a large piece of broken tile on the chair that would fall and smash on the stone floor if anyone tried to force their way inside. That way I would get more of a warning, and hopefully, the tile smashing would wake me up if I was asleep.

Julia would have to call out to me when she came so that I could remove the tile and the chair to let her in. She would also know that someone uninvited was inside if she arrived and found the chair removed and the tile smashed, and then she would have to leave in a hurry. I hoped that Alfonso's visit was just a one off thing, but somehow I doubted it. We knew he was in love with Julia and he might well decide to spend an afternoon sleeping on her mattress again sometime soon.

*

Fortunately, Alfonso didn't return over the next few days and Julia and I relaxed slightly although I always replaced the chair under the door handle once she was safely inside with me. We spent as much time as possible together and I liked nothing better than to lie next to her on her mattress and spend the siesta hours lazily stroking her small breasts, it was something I never tired of.

One morning when I awoke early, I set off for her aunt's farm and hid along the track watching her go about her daily chores. I daydreamed that one day we might live together on a little farm and look after a few animals and grow vegetables. It was a nice idea. All thoughts of going to university had completely left my mind. All I wanted to do was make Julia happy, which I knew would in turn make me happy too.

She didn't come to the venta that day, there were some days when she just couldn't get away, but I was happy that I had seen her even though she hadn't seen me.

I had made a start on repairing the roof. I wasn't very confident about what I was doing, but I was determined to have a go. I tackled the job by standing on top of her father's old chest of drawers which was the tallest item of furniture I could find. The first thing to do was to repair the wooden interior structure from the inside and then go up onto the roof to replace the tiles that were missing. I wasn't looking forward to going up onto the roof, but I was determined to do it.

*

Julia came one morning with some news of the war, the same war I had come to fight in and forgotten so completely. She said that Alfonso's father who had a radio and listened to Franco's Radio Nacional de España had told her father what was being reported. The Republican attack across the River Ebro had stalled in front of Gandesa which they had failed to capture. The town was under siege, but more and more Nationalist reinforcements were arriving every day. It was terrible news. The great battle to turn the tide of the war had failed to take its major objective.

Gandesa had been seen as an essential target since it was an important communication hub, and without it the Republican advance was never likely to succeed. I comforted myself with the thought that Franco's radio might not be telling the whole truth, but even so I wondered how many of those who had crossed the Ebro with me had already died. I felt a profound sense of guilt and shame.

Corbera had fallen quickly but the attack on Gandesa had stalled in the Sierra Caballs according to what Julia had learnt from her father. Now the most likely outcome was that the Republic would carry out a fighting retreat until its shattered Army of the Ebro was forced back across the river. I realised that the war could sweep back through where we were at any moment. The thought terrified me, not so much with fear of what might happen to me, but with a terrible realisation that I was seriously putting Julia's life at risk. I talked to her about it. I could still try to rejoin my unit. I could say that I had been injured or captured by the enemy, but they were unlikely to take me back into the fold without a fuss. I would probably be shot as a deserter. Julia was determined that I shouldn't leave.

We decided that if the war returned I would find somewhere to hide out in the hills and wait for it to go away again. I was worried by the thought of a retreating brigade stumbling across Julia's aunt's farm, but she insisted that it was safe. I was sure she said that so as not to worry me. I would have to try to hide out nearby in case I was needed. Julia said she would start to store up supplies for me for when the time came, some food and a blanket and plenty of water.

We lived on our nerves for a few days, but the siege of Gandesa continued and there was no Nationalist counter attack to relieve the pressure. Julia and I went up into the hills beyond the farm, following winding goat tracks all over the place to try to find a suitable shelter for me, but there was nowhere obvious. It was a bleak landscape away from the little fertile valley where the two farms nestled together, lost to the world. I told her not to worry, that I would find somewhere when the time came.

*

The end of the siege of Gandesa happened suddenly and quickly in the first few days of September. On the 4th, Corbera was recaptured and Julia came running to the venta to tell me that the time had come to escape into the hills. She arrived panting and out of breath and grabbed me by the arm to pull me out of the house. I broke away and went down to the cellar to get my things which I wrapped up in one of the dusty old curtains I had used to cover me. Then we raced along the track away from the buildings. We hadn't gone far when we heard the sound of approaching gunfire quickly followed by the drone of an aircraft. We kept running and didn't stop until we were close to the farm.

"Wait here," she told me and pointed to a clump of bushes. "I'll get back as soon as I can."

I lay face down under the bushes trying to make myself as invisible as possible and listened to the noise of the war that had finally decided to return to haunt us. Suddenly, a little way off, I heard the sound of someone running along the track towards my hiding place, their boots striking the rocks and slithering across the loose stones in their haste to get away from the fighting. I watched in horror as a young man in a Republican uniform came into view. His face was full of fear and he was gulping air into his lungs as he ran for his life. As he drew level with my hiding place, a shot rang out and he seemed to trip over something on the path and tumbled to the ground. I saw his head jolt back upwards as it hit a small rock and then drop back down again. He coughed quietly and blood began to flow out of his open mouth whilst I looked into his staring eyes. I'm not sure if he could see me or not as he lay there dying, if he could it must have been terribly confusing for him.

The soldier who had been chasing him walked slowly along the track, his rifle pointing down at the man he had shot. He stood over him for a few seconds until the man stopped his quiet coughing and lay still. The Rebel soldier kicked him in the side and the body rose slightly and fell back into the dust. The man muttered something under his breath which I didn't catch and then turned to walk back down the track. Had he looked over at the bushes he would surely have seen me, but he had been too wrapped up in his victim lying dead in the dirt.

When I was sure the Fascist had gone, I dashed out from my hiding place to grab the dead man's rifle and an ammunition pouch. Just as I returned to the bushes

I heard Julia calling my name. I looked over at her and saw her running towards the body lying in the middle of the track. She must have assumed it was me. She had dropped the basket containing my emergency supplies. I sprang out onto the track so that she could see that I was very much alive.

She reached me and threw herself into my arms. I realised she was sobbing, her tiny body heaving against mine. Quickly she pulled herself away and looked at me and saw the rifle in my hand.

"You shot him?" she asked.

"No. There was a Fascist soldier chasing him. I just took his rifle."

She looked down at the body.

"We need to move him out of sight," she decided, "quickly before anyone else comes." She was right of course. I slung the rifle over my shoulder, pocketed the ammunition pouch and lifted my dead comrade up off the ground. Julia took a hold too and between us we managed to drag him over to the bushes where I had been hiding. We left him there covered by the old curtain I had brought from the venta and went back towards the farm to collect my supplies which were littered everywhere.

I helped Julia scoop up the pears and tomatoes and pieces of bread and chorizo that had fallen out of her basket and we quickly stuffed them back under the blanket she had found for me.

"Quick, go now," she told me handing me the basket. I knew she was worried that another rebel soldier might come down the track or even a whole platoon, or that someone from her family might have heard the shooting and come out to investigate. I hesitated, wanting to look into her eyes just once more in case I never had the chance to do so again.

"Go," she shouted.

"I love you," I told her.

"I know," she said and she pushed me away. I fled up a steep slope and hurried out of sight into a dip on the other side. Then I ran along some flat ground and then over another rise. I kept going until I reckoned I had by-passed the farm, so I turned and headed back towards it. It didn't take long for me to find it again. I spotted a good place to hide, amongst some trees, just out of sight. I sat down and just listened. I don't know what I thought I would do if an enemy squad found the farm, but I checked that my rifle was loaded and held it up as if taking aim to feel its weight. I decided that I would try to go down fighting, that's what my father would have done.

When it grew dark, I went to the pear trees at the top terrace and covering my shoulders with the blanket I leant back against a tree trunk to do sentry duty. In the early hours of the morning I must have fallen asleep. I awoke to the sound of the cock's first cry and retreated quickly back up to my hiding place of the previous afternoon.

All through that morning, I could hear the sounds of gunfire coming from the direction of the venta. I thought that our retreating army must be trying to make a stand there. Sometime, around midday, a pair of black aircraft appeared overhead, lazily circling the Sierras like tired flies, looking for somewhere to dump their bombs. I saw them start to dive but then I lost them from view beyond a nearby peak. I few seconds later I heard the sound of explosions rattling through the ravines and valleys towards me, bouncing off the cliff faces and boulders. I thought about the venta's roof that I had been repairing and wondered why I had bothered.

Sporadic fire continued into the late afternoon, but by nightfall there was silence. I crept down to the pear trees once again and took up my lonely vigil. Who knew what might happen. It was a terribly confusing time.

CHAPTER TWELVE

When the cock crowed the next morning, I waited for Julia to emerge from the little farmhouse to go about her daily chores. I called out to her as she walked across to the pigsty and she turned to see me waving at her. She quickly threw the pig its breakfast and then ran up the sloping farm terraces to see me. She arrived out of breath and grabbed my face with both hands pulling my lips to hers.

"I'm so glad you're alive," she panted. "I've been worried sick."

"I wasn't far away," I told her. She saw my blanket on the ground next to a pear tree.

"You were hiding up here?"

"No, not during the day. I only came here at night to keep watch."

"Well, you should leave in case my aunt comes out."

"I know. I just wanted to see you, that's all."

She smiled at me and looked deeply into my eyes. I'd missed the way she did that.

"Come back here tonight when it gets dark," she whispered, "I'll get out of my bedroom window."

I spent the day higher up the hillside, half asleep, ears straining for the sounds of war, but none came. I hoped that the war had finally forgotten about us. I wondered if the venta had been destroyed or if I could go back to living there.

As it began to grow dark, I made my way back to the pear tree terrace. Once there, I sat to wait for Julia. It was a long while before I heard movement down below. Someone was picking their way carefully, almost silently, up from the farm towards me. My heart began to beat faster as it always did at the prospect of seeing Julia.

At last, peering into the darkness, I caught a glimpse of the girl, ghost-like in a filmy cotton nightdress. She was barefoot so as not to make a sound and she was delicately threading her way upwards from terrace to terrace.

When she finally arrived we kissed and then she stepped back from me. She gave me a shy smile and began to lift her nightdress slowly up and then over her head. She dropped it at her feet and stood there naked before me. I just looked at her. It was what she seemed to want me to do. The faint moon gave her pale skin a glow that made her look like an angel. After a while, I noticed that she had goose-bumps on her arms and I stepped towards her and held her close to me.

When I awoke sometime in the night she was gone and I lay alone on the blanket my teeth chattering with the cold. It was at that moment that I realised that autumn was on its way, that I wouldn't be able to sleep outside much longer. I hoped that I would be able to return to the venta the next day.

At dawn, still shivering, I waited for Julia to come out. She fed the pig and I scrambled down to meet her.

"I was so cold that I had to go back inside," she whispered.

"I was shivering all night," I told her. "I want to go back to the venta today."

"Okay. Wait along the track and I'll come with you around mid-morning."

*

We found the venta in ruins. Julia clasped her hand over her mouth and started to cry. I held her tightly to me and tried to comfort her, but there was nothing I could say. Eventually, we started to scramble across the rubble and found that the rear wall of the house was still standing. We went out to the patio and sat on the wall of the well.

"We'll never leave the farm now," said the girl. "This will never be our home again. My father will be devastated."

"It can be rebuilt," I told her.

"We don't have the money to get it rebuilt. This was all we had." She burst into tears once more.

An hour or so later, we went to look around at the other houses, but it was the same story, the bombs had half-destroyed them all. Only a few fragile walls remained here and there shrouded in a fine mist of dust. Apart from the ruined buildings, other evidence remained of the desperate fight that had taken place there a few days before. We saw some spent cartridge cases and a few broken weapons and bits of discarded uniform. The bodies had been removed, but there were several patches of dried blood or dried brains that clearly indicated where men had fallen. I found a boot with a foot still inside it, but I managed to steer Julia away before she saw it.

The idyllic existence we had shared together had been shattered. My hopes of staying at the venta until the end of the war and then of building a life with Julia were dashed. I couldn't think what to do. In the end, the only place left for me to sleep was the venta's dark cellar, but it was by no means ideal. Come the winter it would be unbearably cold down there. I found Julia's mattress amid the rubble and pulled it out for me to sleep on. I had my blanket and it would be better than sleeping out in the open.

I carried on that way for a few days, trying to come to terms with my new living conditions. Julia would come to bring me food as she always had done and we would snatch a few more precious moments together, but things were not like they had been before. We both knew that I wouldn't be able to continue to live in the cellar when the first snows came. My leg was more or less healed although it still felt a bit stiff in the mornings. I could walk well enough, but I couldn't think where I could walk to. There was also an ugly scar across my forehead that would always serve as a reminder of my idiotic Spanish escapade whatever happened to me in later life. I was growing my fringe long to try to hide it.

*

Late one afternoon, Julia and I were asleep down in the cellar. We were naked under the blanket, embraced together. The girl should have left long ago, but she hadn't. Suddenly, I was awoken by the sound of a falling stone somewhere above us. I woke the girl with my hand over her mouth so that she didn't say anything and give us away. She sensed my alarm and we lay very still listening. There was more movement up above. Someone was slowly clambering across the rubble.

Julia leapt to her feet and began to pull her dress on. I jumped into my trousers and was just doing them up when we heard shuffling at the top of the stairs. Something moved across to block off the light and then we heard steps beginning to descend. The girl screamed.

"Julia, are you there?" came a male voice. We saw someone coming slowly down the flight of stone steps, descending with difficulty.

"Alfonso, what are you doing here?" snapped the girl trying to puff out her chest and make herself as large as possible.

"I should ask you that," was the reply. Alfonso reached the bottom of the steps and peered into the semi-darkness of the cellar. It took a moment for his eyes to adjust, but when he saw me standing next to Julia he was visibly shocked.

"Who's that?" he asked.

"He's a wounded soldier," she told him, "I've been looking after him."

"Is he a Red?"

At that moment, I remembered my rifle across the cellar behind the low wall and I made a dash for it. I reached down and grabbed it, released the safety and quickly brought it up to my shoulder. I aimed at Alfonso but I didn't shoot. I don't know why I couldn't pull the trigger at that moment. I should have done.

"Don't shoot," shouted Julia which added to my confusion. "Go Alfonso. Just go and never come back here," she shouted at him. He didn't need to be told twice and he turned away and fumbled his way back up the steps. I followed him with my rifle but again I didn't shoot. When he reached the top I had my last opportunity to fire, but I continued to hesitate and then he was gone. We heard him stumbling across the debris of the bombed-out venta, falling, cursing and picking himself up and stumbling on again, desperate to get away.

"Will he tell anyone about me?" I asked although I knew the answer.

"He's on his way to tell my father for sure. He's going to kill me."

"You should leave now. I've got to go too. I can't risk him giving me away. Besides, if they find you here with me they'll shoot you."

I realised that she was crying. She leant towards me, rested her forehead against mine, and looked deep into my eyes. It was always a heady experience when she did that, but this time with her shiny tears it tore my heart apart.

"It's too dark for me to get home now," she decided "and it's too dark for you to get anywhere. We should stay here for the night and set off early in the morning."

"You're crazy," I told her. "We've got to leave right away."

"I want to spend the night with you," she whispered. "We'll get up before dawn, no one will come before it's light."

I knew it was madness. I knew it was the last chance for me to save us, but I couldn't tear myself away from her, not at that moment, it was too sudden. It would have been like a death. Somewhat reluctantly I agreed that we should spend a last few hours together and part at dawn. I didn't really have much of an idea as to what to do, and the only thing I could think of was heading for the river and trying to find a way across back to my own lines. It was a useless and scary plan, one with almost no chance of success, but it was all I had.

I hated to leave the girl to her fate, but I would just have to hope that her father would forgive her, eventually.

"I'll come back and find you," I told her, "I promise. One day when the war is over." She reached up and put a finger over my lips.

"Don't make promises," she whispered and she kissed me and we lay down together on the mattress in the darkness of the cellar and held each other as tightly as we could, hoping I think that this last night would last forever.

CHAPTER THIRTEEN

The end, when it came was sharp and sudden. We must have fallen asleep wrapped together, although it had been our intention to stay awake all night. The girl shook me. It was still dark. I didn't need to ask her what the matter was because I heard the unmistakeable sound of boots clambering over the rubble of the venta above us. And it wasn't just one person either, that was obvious. Someone cursed quietly. It was all over. I didn't bother to reach for my weapon which was lying by my side. If I started shooting they would just drop a grenade into the cellar and that would be that.

"I love you," I whispered at her mouth in the darkness which I knew was there because I could feel her hot ragged breathing.

"I know," she whispered back and she held me as tightly as she could and I heard her crying softly. I saw the thin shaft of a torch beam at the opening to the cellar and heard the bolt of a rifle being drawn back. I pulled off our blanket and stood up slowly and then helped Julia to her feet keeping her behind my back.

Someone blocked off the pale moonlight at the open entrance to the cellar and the groping finger of the torch beam reached around the darkness until it found us. A second dark shape appeared above us and a second thin beam of light shone into my eyes.

"Come out slowly," said a voice. I lead Julia carefully up the stone steps into the fresh air. As soon as we emerged we were snatched apart. I was thrown down to the ground and thoroughly searched. My hands were quickly tied with rope and then I was hauled to my feet. Someone approached from the darkness. I realised it was Alfonso.

"That's him," he said in a high-pitched excited voice, although it must have been obvious that I was the enemy soldier he had told them about. So he hadn't gone to Julia's father as she had thought he would, instead he had gone straight to the Nationalists and by so doing he had condemned not only me but also the girl.

He obviously hadn't been that in love with her, or perhaps he just couldn't stand the thought that she loved another. Maybe this was some sort of revenge for her constant rejections. Did he hope that the Fascists would take revenge not only on the girl but also against her family? If these men went to the farm and killed everyone they found there, then Alfonso's family could just take over the land with no fuss.

I should have shot him when I had the chance, I realised that now. We could have buried his body in the rubble, I could have escaped and Julia could have gone back to the farm. If I had somehow made it out of Spain alive, although I didn't have a clue as to how

I might have achieved that, then I could have come back for her some day. Maybe the war would be over in a couple of years and I could just return to join her and we could work out some sort of life together. It was easy to think that way, being so young anything seemed possible.

The two men began to lead me away across the debris of the fallen walls of the venta, holding my arms so tightly that it hurt, pushing and shoving me although there was no need, I wasn't putting up any sort of resistance. I wondered if they would just walk me over to the road and finish it with a quick bullet to the brain.

"Martin," I heard the girl call out, "I love you." It was long and drawn out, loud in the silence of the night, like the slow screech of a dying owl.

"I know," I shouted back. One of my guards crashed the butt of his rifle into my shoulder blades and I fell over onto the smashed up stones over which we were walking. With my hands tied I couldn't break my fall and I landed on my face and chest. They hauled me back to my feet and we set off once more for the road. I felt blood on my right cheek, but what did that matter now? As I was led away my ears strained for the sound of a shot that might signal the end of the girl's life.

The soldiers shoved me roughly over the remains of the low wall by the road and then we stood and waited. They didn't tell me to kneel down to make a shot in the head easier instead one of them produced a crumpled pack of cigarettes. Was this the last smoke for a condemned man? He offered one to the other soldier who took it and then fumbled in his pocket for matches. They lit their cigarettes and started to smoke. My heart was beating so fast it felt like it might explode. If these were my last moments on earth I was determined to face up to them bravely. I didn't want the girl, still somewhere out there in the darkness nearby, to hear me crying for my mother or something when the time came.

I was surprised that I wasn't offered a cigarette. I didn't smoke and I wouldn't have wanted one, but the offer was sort of expected. I stood there, head bowed and the two soldiers stood beside me smoking silently. I realised it was quite cold but that just made me feel more alive. Funny that I should feel so alive when I was so close to death.

Out of the darkness, away along the road, I heard the approach of a lorry. The sound grew louder and finally a pair of dim headlights came into view. The old engine rattled and coughed and its progress was slow. I realised now why we were waiting at the roadside. Either, I would be bundled into the lorry and taken somewhere else for interrogation and execution, or an officer would get out of the cab, draw his revolver and do the necessary deed himself. I took a deep breath of the cold pre-dawn air and felt it fizzing in my lungs.

The lorry arrived in a tired screech of brakes and a wheeze of exhaust. The officer I had been expecting jumped down from the cab and peered closely at my face.

"Is this him?" he asked obviously disappointed by my appearance. What had been expecting? "He's just a kid."

"He's been hiding here in a cellar," said one of my guards as if that would somehow make up for them having obviously wasted their time.

"Shoot him," barked the officer and he turned to get back to the warmth of the cab.

"I'm English," I called out to him, "inglés." I don't know why I thought that might help me, but it was all I could come up with. He stopped and turned back to look at me. It was a long slow observation as he took me in from head to toe. I didn't look Spanish that was for sure, I had inherited my father's blonde hair and it must have been obvious even in the slim light of that early hour. He nodded slightly. I realised that I had succeeded in capturing his interest.

"Stick him in the back," he ordered. I breathed a huge sigh of relief. I knew it was only a temporary reprieve, but I was glad that they wouldn't just dispatch me there by the roadside for the girl to see. My guards dropped the tailgate of the lorry, bundled me inside and climbed in after. They picked me up and put me on a wooden bench seat. One of them sat beside me and the other settled himself on the other side on a similar bench.

The lorry set off jolting and shaking along the unmade road. I felt myself bouncing from side to side matching the bumps of the track. My two silent sentinels bounced too, the ash falling from their dying cigarettes. I tried to see out of the opening in the tarpaulin at the rear, desperate to catch a last glimpse of the girl, but I couldn't see her. I supposed that the other soldiers would just shoot her there amidst the ruins of the only home she had ever known.

*

We hadn't gone far when one of my guards produced a hipflask from his jacket pocket. He took a quick gulp and offered it to his companion. The other man drank and then began to splutter and cough.

"What's this shit?" he asked.

"Good, isn't it?" laughed the other one reaching for the flask and taking another shot.

"Tastes like horse piss," came the reply. But, when it was offered to him again, he accepted it without protest and took a second longer drink.

I guessed that they were relieved to be alive. They had been sent out on some bizarre early morning mission to capture a hidden enemy soldier who they would have assumed to be armed and desperate. They had been just as scared of meeting me as I had been all this time at the prospect of meeting them. Now it was over and they were glad to have survived. I wasn't the terrible enemy that they had feared. I was just a terrified foreign kid who had somehow stumbled into a man's war. How I had managed it they didn't know and didn't care. What would happen to me was no concern of theirs either, they would have shot me back at the venta and thought nothing of it. It was a war, a civil war, people died for little or no reason all the time.

The sun came up and I saw the countryside through which we were passing, the same bleak landscape that hugged the low sierras where the great River Ebro carved its weary trail. I had no idea where they might be taking me. My knowledge of the geography of Spain was almost non-existent so even if they had mentioned the name of some town or city it wouldn't have meant anything to me at that time. Apart from Madrid and Barcelona the only other city I had heard of was Seville and I knew that that was a long way to the south.

*

About half an hour after we set off, I noticed that the man sitting opposite me had nodded off to sleep his head back against the tarpaulin side of the lorry. They must have been woken at four in the morning or even earlier, and with the addition of some strong alcohol exhaustion had taken over. I turned to look at the man beside me and saw his head start to fall slowly forward towards his chest. A sudden jolt, and he lifted his head back up instantly, but it wasn't long before I saw his eyes close and his head dropping once more. I looked out of the back of the lorry. We were climbing a steady slope with rocks on both sides and trees beyond that.

I knew that this was the moment to escape. If I didn't go now I would never get another chance. I got slowly and silently to my feet and stood between the two soldiers careful not to touch them as the lorry swayed. When I was sure I hadn't been detected I took a step towards the rear and then I paused and waited again. My guards slumbered on, exhausted soldiers in an exhausting war. I took another step and then another and I had reached the tailgate at the back of the lorry. I peered out through the gap in the tarpaulin willing myself to jump while I had the chance. I was scared, terribly scared. I knew that if they caught me I would be shot instantly, but I also knew that if I didn't escape I was going to be shot at some stage anyway.

I tried to jump over the tailgate, but in the end it was just an ungainly fall. I crashed to the ground and despite my efforts to keep quiet I let out a loud cry of pain as I landed on my right shoulder. I had tried to twist in the air to avoid landing on my face, but the fall from the moving lorry to the hard stones of the track was painful enough anyway. Instantly I pushed myself up, despite my tied hands, and I was off and running. My heart pounded blood to my legs and I sprinted faster than I would ever have believed possible.

I heard shouting from the lorry and the squeal of its brakes, but by then I was off the track and through the boulders and into the trees. I wasn't going to stop for anything in the world. I heard the crack of a rifle but no bullet came and it only spurred me on to run even faster.

I fled, zigzagging through the oak trees, gasping for air and willing my legs to keep going. I didn't care in which direction I might be heading, the only important thing was to put as great a distance as possible between myself and my captors. There came a time when I began to feel sick, when I felt my legs about to give way beneath me, but I pushed on further still. Eventually, everything started to shake all around me as I grew dizzy and then I just collapsed, exhausted to the ground.

I lay in a little hollow between two tall oaks and tried to quieten the sound of my breathing to try to hear what was around me. I wasn't sure how long I had been running, it had seemed like hours, but probably it wasn't that long. I wondered how hard they would look for me. I didn't imagine that they thought me to be incredibly important in the overall scheme of the war, and so I hoped that they wouldn't search for me too hard. They probably assumed that I would die in the woods within a few days.

CHAPTER FOURTEEN

I lay where I had fallen. It seemed to take forever for my body to stop shaking and my breathing to return to almost normal. My heart still pounded in my chest like it was a drum. I heard nothing except for the sounds of the forest, birds squabbling and insects yawning, the breeze through the leaves of the oak trees. I was curled up on my side in the dappled shade like a cowering fox waiting for the hounds which he could no longer outrun. I stayed there, willing myself to be silent, my ears straining for the sound of approaching men. After several hours I fell asleep and when I awoke I was cold and alone and probably safe. It was dark.

I picked myself up and looked around for some way to cut the rope that still held my hands. In the end, I tried rubbing the rope across the jagged edge of a boulder and eventually I managed to break it. My wrists were sore and my shoulder ached but I was glad to have escaped. I sat down on the boulder and thought about the girl. I knew in my heart that she was dead. There was no other possible outcome. She had helped an enemy soldier, sheltered him and bathed his wounds and brought him food, and she had been there beside him when he was captured. She must have known what would happen, and yet she had let it happen. I wondered at the mighty power of love. How had it made us take risks that we knew would get us both killed? And yet we had taken them. We had known that it would end this way but we had refused to believe it.

Those days spent with Julia had seemed to me to have given reason to my existence. I felt that I hadn't been put on earth for any other cause except to have known her at that precise time. I held my head in my hands and wept. I felt so terrible that really I would have preferred to have been shot back at the venta rather than to have to face the rest of my life without her. Without her, but with the burden of knowing that I could so easily have saved her, and I hadn't.

At daybreak, I got to my feet and began to slowly move about. I wasn't sure what to do or where to go. Eventually, I decided that if I stayed in the forest I would certainly perish. I might get attacked at night by wolves or simply starve to death lying between the oak trees. It was best to try to get back to the road. Someone brought up in the country might have been able to survive in that forest, eating berries and roots and setting traps for rabbits and tree rats, but I didn't know anything about that. At my school they had taught us to play rugby and cricket, to do algebra and to recite poetry. I had beautiful handwriting and had read four Shakespeare plays but all of that was of no use whatsoever to me now.

I blundered about for most of the day, probably going around in circles, and then I found a small clearing and settled down to wait for nightfall. I would have liked to have started a fire, it would have made me feel a bit safer, but of course I didn't know how to. In the darkest hours of the night the moon disappeared and it started to rain. I sat there miserable and shivering and tortured myself with thoughts of the girl's warm skin pressed against me and the gentle calm of her breathing and I cried wretchedly once more form despair, loneliness and guilt.

It was late the next afternoon that, by chance, I stumbled across a track cutting through the forest. It wasn't the road I had been looking for, but it must lead somewhere. I followed it downhill just because the going looked easier and because it might lead down to a river valley and I was desperately thirsty.

By nightfall I hadn't found the river and I sorted out somewhere to curl up for the night between some boulders. It was yet another miserable night. Once more it rained heavily and I lay there with my mouth open to try to get some sort of relief for my terrible thirst. After the rain stopped, I lay on the ground soaked and shivering until dawn.

When the sun finally started to rise, I realised that the forest was shrouded in a heavy autumnal fog. I licked some water from the lowest leaves of the trees and then set off once more. In normal circumstances the going might not have been so difficult, but I was exhausted and after just a couple of hours walking, my head became light and seemed to swim through the air. My vision was beginning to blur and the colours and shapes of the forest around me seemed to merge together. I was sweating and shivering at the same time.

Suddenly, I collapsed to the ground as without warning my legs just buckled beneath me. I lay there in the middle of the path looking up at the shifting sky, my mind in turmoil. It would have been easy to have given up at that moment, and to be honest there have been times in later life when I have wished that I had done so, but after resting for a while I forced myself to continue once more. I walked slowly, head bowed, my eyes closed for long periods to stop the dizziness from creeping up on me again.

Then I remember falling. I had stumbled over a rocky cliff that I hadn't seen and tumbled down a steep little slope before landing with a splash in a stream at the bottom. The cold water brought me to my senses and I sat there for a long while taking deep breaths and telling myself that I shouldn't give up. This stream was my way out, a thin lifeline to salvation.

I drank some cold water and then stripped off my clothes, washed the mud out of them and lay them on the rocks of the bank to dry in the sun now that the fog had lifted. I cleaned my boots and then my body. As I ran my wet hands over myself, I realised just how terribly thin I had become. I had felt close to starvation from the moment I had arrived in Spain, but here lost in the forest, I knew that I would soon be suffering from malnutrition.

I sat shivering in the weak sun beside my clothes and waited for some sort of warmth to return to my body. I did feel a little better now. I had had a good drink of water and a wash and I had convinced myself that there was a way out of my situation. The stream could lead to a river and the river could take me back to humanity. Of course there would be a whole new set of problems waiting for me if I did manage to regain contact with people, but I would have to face them when the time came. My priorities now were food and shelter. I knew for certain that I couldn't survive the winter in the forest. I would freeze to death with the first snows.

I pulled on my damp but clean clothes in the middle of the afternoon and set off following the flow of the stream. When I got tired I took a quick drink and sat down to rest and then carried on again. In this way, come dusk I felt that I had made some good progress although I was still surrounded by forest. I curled myself up into a tight ball and spent the night cursing my summer uniform and wishing that I had left the venta as planned with a blanket and a jumper and of course some food.

As soon as it was light enough to see, I was off again trying to get warm. After a few hours I realised that the forest was starting to thin out a bit and soon I came to a valley where the stream joined a river. The river was low at this time of year and there was a wide dried-up flood plain which was easy to walk along. Come the spring melt it would be a huge torrent of surging water, but now it was solid ground baked hard by the summer.

After a day of walking, with my stomach twisting at my guts, I suddenly came upon a little hut perched on a cliff top overlooking the river valley. There was a thin wisp of smoke shimmering upwards through a hole in the roof and I swore I could smell something cooking. My head told me to bypass this place and continue downriver, but my stomach was crying out for something to fill its gnawing emptiness. I had no choice but to throw myself upon the mercy of whoever might be in the hut. They could be Fascist soldiers hunting for stragglers in the forest, but at the moment I just didn't care.

I used my last reserves of energy to scramble up the slope and quietly crept round to the front of the hut. The door was hanging off its hinges and I saw an old man sitting on a three-legged stool feeding twigs to a small fire. Above the fire a blackened cooking pot was hanging and whatever was inside it was beginning to heat up, releasing a potent aroma of herbs and maybe rabbit. I didn't care what it was I just knew I had to have some. It was all I could do to stop myself from bursting into the hut and snatching the pot from the fire and pouring its delicious contents straight down my throat.

The old man suddenly became aware of my presence and shot upright from his stool with an agility that took me by surprise. He reached for an old hunting rifle that was propped up against the wall and quickly levelled it at me pointing it at my chest.

I guess I must have passed out from exhaustion because the next thing I remember was the old man trying to force some of his watery soup into my mouth with a bent up spoon. The soup burned my lips and scalded the top of my mouth, but it made me feel alive. I sat there with my back against the damp wooden wall whilst the old man fed me his tasteless broth until it was all gone. He left me then and took the pot and began to gnaw at the tiny rabbit bones that were all that remained.

"Where have you come from boy?" he asked me when he had finished eating.

"I was wounded in a battle," I told him, "then I got lost in the forest."

"You don't look like a soldier," he said suspiciously. His accent was thick and hard and difficult for me to understand. I saw him running his eyes over my uniform as if trying to decide on which side I might have been fighting. "Are you a Fascist?"

"No."

"So you're a Red then."

"Not really."

"So what are you?"

"Lost. Lost in the forest."

"You're a deserter."

"Maybe. Does it matter?"

"Guess not. How long have you been in the forest?"

"A few days."

"My son went to the war. Never came back."

"Communist?" I asked hoping that we were at least on the same side.

"Anarchist," spat the old man as if he hated the word. "Told him not to go. Told him he'd get himself killed."

The old man got to his feet and came over to take a closer look at me, it was getting dark now.

"You can sleep here tonight," he told me.

"Thanks," I mumbled in reply and I just closed my eyes.

*

When I awoke in the morning I was alone. The old man had set off early and hadn't bothered to say goodbye. I wondered if he had gone to fetch the Civil Guard or something. There might be a small reward offered for turning in deserters, even enemy ones. I decided not to hang around. Whatever he might have been, Fascist, Communist, Anarchist or any other name you care to give him, the truth is that the old man who I stumbled across by chance had saved my life.

A thin mist hung over the river that morning, I remember thinking that it was better than the fog of the previous day, and I pushed through it with determination. The river had now cut itself a deep gorge and the hillsides towered above me. I was so alone that I felt like the only person remaining left alive. When I sat down by the river's edge to rest around midday, I saw a deer come to drink a little upstream on the opposite bank. If I had been carrying a rifle I couldn't have missed it, but as it was I could only sit and marvel at its graceful beauty.

Sometime in the afternoon, I came across a little abandoned farm. I searched the house frantically for anything edible but there was nothing, however just behind the house was an old pear tree and I was able to climb it and get some half-ripe fruit from the upper branches. I sat at the foot of the tree and quickly ate all but the hardest of the little pears I had gathered. I had been lucky for the second day running. That night I slept in the farmhouse on the kitchen table safe from the scurrying rats on the floor below.

CHAPTER FIFTEEN

With two pocketfuls of hard pears I left the farmhouse at dawn. The table where I had slept although away from the rats had not been very comfortable. I was stiff and it took a while for my body to get going again. Once more there was a mist hanging over the river. The air was cold and heavy.

The gorge through which I had been walking suddenly came to an end and my little river poured itself into a wide expanse of water that I guessed must be the Ebro. So I was back where I had started from. I could only hope that the far bank was still in our hands. My problem now was how to get across to safety.

There was no one around anywhere to be seen. Either, I had found a forgotten gap in the lines or I had walked out of the battle zone altogether. Perhaps the Civil War had raged off somewhere else and left the Ebro front in peace for a while.

I sat down in a clump of bushes and watched the mighty flow of the river surging past. I wasn't a strong swimmer so I decided that I would most likely drown if I tried to swim to the far side. Then I noticed a tree trunk stuck between some rocks close by. It must have been floating down the river and got caught up. I pushed it out away from the rocks and splashed in after it as it began to bob and weave in the current. I clung onto the trunk as best I could and kicked hard with my legs hoping to get over to the other side.

The surge of the water was stronger than I had expected or perhaps I was just weaker than I had thought because I made little or no progress across the river, instead I was being carried downstream against my will. I could have let go of the tree trunk and swum back to the bank, but in the end I decided to hold on and just go where the waters took me.

It was a crazy feeling to find myself being sucked along by the strength of the current with nothing I could do about it. I held onto the soaked wood for all I was worth and tried to keep my head above water as much as possible.

There came a time when my arms grew weak with cramp and cold and I thought I might just give up, but somehow I kept hold until eventually the river widened and the current stilled. At last I was able to swim towards the other side. As soon as I could feel the stony river bed beneath my feet, I waded out and threw myself down on the grassy bank to recover. I ate a couple of hard pears. I was shivering uncontrollably, so I knew that I had to start walking in order to get some warmth back into my body. I really needed to find some shelter before nightfall.

After a short walk I found a track that led alongside the river and I followed it until I came to a little village. A boy was sitting abandoned by the roadside in the late evening sunshine. He stood up when he heard me approaching.

"Have you come from the war?" he called out.

"Yes. What's the name of this place?" I asked. He did tell me the name, but it didn't mean anything to me and I've since forgotten it. It could have been anywhere.

"Am I in the Republican Zone?" I asked him.

"Yes Comrade," he responded raising a clenched fist in official greeting. I breathed a huge sigh of relief.

"Take me to the Town Hall," I told him and we set off with him leading me into the village. It wasn't really very big, a few narrow streets with the houses on opposite sides almost touching each other. As we walked toward the centre, people stopped to stare at me. I must have been a terrible sight having lived wild in the woods for so many days. Maybe they thought I had come to tell them that the war was lost.

The boy took me to a small rundown stone building which looked official because it had a Republican flag flying at the top of a rusty pole. It was being used as a sort of makeshift headquarters for some sort of local militia. There was a guard seated on a bench outside who got lazily to his feet when he saw me, picking his rifle up.

"What have we here?" he asked.

"He's from the war, I found him," said the boy puffing out his chest with pride.

The soldier looked at me in disbelief. He took in my torn and ragged uniform, my dishevelled appearance and my strange blonde hair. I must have seemed like some alien creature descended from another planet.

"Are you a soldier?" he asked eventually.

"Yes, Comrade, I'm from the 16th Battalion, XV International Brigade."

"International Brigade? Where are you from?"

"From England."

He nodded at me as if that explained everything. "You'd better come in," he decided and he stepped aside to allow me to enter the building.

In the semi-darkness of the interior I saw an older man sitting behind a desk that was far too big for him. He looked up when he heard our boots on the stone floor.

"What's up?" he asked.

"This soldier has just turned up," said the other man.

"Is he armed?"

"I don't think so, I'll check."

The man who had been on guard put his rifle down against the wall and came over to give me a pat down.

He found a few small hard pears in my trouser pockets and placed them on the desk. It was obvious that I wasn't dangerous.

"Sit down," the older man told me indicating a high-backed wooden chair. The guard left.

"Thank you, Comrade," I said.

"So, you're a deserter then?" he began.

I spent the next hour sitting there answering a hundred questions that he dreamt up for me. I was exhausted and hungry, but I concentrated as hard as I could on my answers since I knew that this little man, local military god that he was, had the power of life and death over me at that moment. If I couldn't convince him that I wasn't a deserter he would just have the guard outside take me for a walk to the outskirts of the village and shoot me. They could throw my body into the great river and no one would care.

He repeated his questions, rephrasing them slightly, changing the order now and again. Sometimes he spoke in a soft friendly voice, sometimes he became angry and menacing. In the end, he came to a halt and decided he'd had enough of my lies for one day. We could start again in the morning.

"I'm hungry," I told him. I was marched out of the cuartel to a little inn opposite and a small plate of leftovers was served up to me by a girl of about fourteen who tried not to look at my face. Then I was locked in one of the upstairs rooms and left alone. There was a bed, a real bed with a mattress that was so soft it felt like a cloud. I stripped off my damp clothes and pulling a blanket over me I was asleep instantly.

*

I was awoken early the next morning, and at first I couldn't remember where I was, but when I had dressed, I was led downstairs and the girl from the night before handed me a piece of bread and I was taken back over to the cuartel.

Once more I sat down on the wooden chair opposite the big desk. I took a bite of the bread whilst I waited for the questions to start.

"I've spoken to someone from Headquarters," said the man in charge. "I managed to get through on the telephone this morning."

"Yes, Comrade."

"They say you've been missing for several weeks."

"That's what I told you last night."

"Yes, yes, I know - you were wounded, captured by the Fascists and then escaped into the forest and crossed back to our side."

"That's right." I hoped at last he was finally starting to believe me.

"I offered to have you shot as a deserter, but they think you might be some sort of Fascist spy, so they'd like to interrogate you for themselves."

I realised that all I had done was escape certain death at the hands of the Fascists and exchanged it for certain death at the hands of my own side. I started to protest my innocence, but he shut me up and said there was nothing more he could do for me. I was sat outside on the wooden bench next to the guard to wait for a lorry that was coming to take me to Headquarters.

*

Headquarters for the Army of the Ebro turned out to be in a bunker just outside of La Figuera. I slept most of the way tied up on the floor in the back of a small lorry. I wasn't going to try to escape any more. It was clear that both sides wanted me dead and I decided to resign myself to my fate. I was tired of running away and tired of always expecting to be caught. I missed Julia terribly and my heart didn't want to live on without her.

I was interrogated by a huge Russian who could have snapped my neck with one of his huge hands without even breaking sweat. I had been worried that I might be tortured to reveal Fascist secrets, but the Russian soon tired of me and left the cell where I was being held. I heard him shouting at someone about having his precious time wasted in the corridor outside and then he was gone. A soldier came with a canteen of rancid stew that was probably the best tasting meal I had in my entire time in the Republican Army and then I was left alone for a couple of days with just a jug of water and a blanket and a little camp bed.

Early on the third morning I was awoken by the sound of a key in the lock. I wondered if my time had finally run out. To my surprise I was handed a small loaf of bread by a young soldier of about my own age and then I was led outside. The sun was just beginning to climb above the distant sierras.

There was a small line of soldiers in filthy uniforms like my own, standing huddled together gnawing at their loaves of bread. A lorry was parked up under a tree and we were told we were being taken to Barcelona to face a military court. We were hounded aboard and forced to sit on the wooden floorboards under armed guard and then the lorry set off.

The journey took most of the day. The lorry was slow and heavy, and creaked and groaned its way out of the sierras and down towards the coast. At Tarragona we stopped for an hour so that the driver and guards could stretch their legs and then we were off again along the coastal road.

Around nightfall, I was back in Barcelona where I had begun my Spanish adventure just a few months earlier - although it seemed like a lifetime ago now. We were driven into the prison and put in shared cells. No one spoke. What was the point of getting to know anyone when we were all condemned men?

*

Every morning as execution hour approached, with a huge stomping of boots, rattling of keys and crashing of doors, the guards would come bursting into the cells and haul out those who had been selected for that day. Some left protesting their innocence, some crying for their mothers, some just went in silence glad that their rotten existence would soon be at an end. From out in the courtyard would come a sharp ripple of gunfire and then quiet would return. That was when you could finally sleep, knowing that you had survived another last night.

Late every afternoon we were given a little bowl of something brown and watery that they said was food, but it smelt and tasted of the sewers. Sometimes, after the morning's executions had been carried out we were given a thin crust of stale bread, but not more than once every two or three days. I realised that we were being slowly starved to death. There were some prisoners who gave up, just curled up on the floor and willed themselves to die.

After I had been there a week, we were taken out en masse to the courtyard and a huge hosepipe was turned on us. Dripping wet and shivering with the cold we were taken back to our cells which had also been hosed down so that our blankets were soaking wet too. That was a miserable day. If they did that to us in the depths of winter they would kill us all, but perhaps that was what they wanted.

After ten or eleven days, by which time I was confused and delirious from hunger, I was suddenly taken to the top floor of the building for my trial. I don't know what I had been expecting, but I was asked about my story and then sentenced to death for being a deserter. The whole charade lasted less than ten minutes. The judge signed my death warrant with a contented swirl of his fountain pen and decreed that the sentence should be carried out as soon as possible.

Back in my cell, I curled myself up into a ball and willed myself to die rather than have to face the firing squad.

CHAPTER SIXTEEN
London, November 1975

I was sitting in my office. I wasn't really doing anything, just sort of wasting time I suppose. I'd been doing a lot of that recently. I was stuck in a bit of a rut. It was the middle of the first term and that's not a happy place to be. I had a pile of papers to mark on my desk and I had the time to do it, I just couldn't motivate myself to pick up the red pen. I tried to argue with myself, if I did it now then I wouldn't have to do it later. I really didn't want to have to take it home with me at the end of the day, did I? Not after having had so much time to get it done during work time.

It was Wednesday, the middle of the week, not a good place to be. Wednesday was marking day. I had a couple of free hours at the end of the morning which I had set aside exclusively for marking work. I didn't use this time for tutorials or for preparing lectures or for writing exams or for chatting with colleagues, this was marking time. But marking time had recently turned into daydreaming time. It was getting worse every week.

At least I had this time to myself. It was nice not to be disturbed for a couple of hours. Had I still felt like writing poetry then it would have been the perfect time to put pen to paper, but I hadn't felt like writing anything for so long that I had begun to accept that I never would again. It didn't bother me that I had long ago lost my inspiration. It didn't bother me that I had also lost my interest in teaching. I was just going through the motions.

At the beginning of each academic year, in one of the first classes of the course for the new intakes, some bright spark would turn up with a copy of my collected poems for me to sign. They always ruined the moment by saying something like "my mum found it in a box in the garage," or "it belonged to my grandmother – she was a big fan." But I would sign it anyway. The students would beg me to read something to them and I would open the slim volume of my collected life's work at random and give them *A Puppet in the Making* regardless of which poem was on the page before me. It was the one that everyone knew, perhaps the only one, even though they were supposed to be English Lit students.

<u>*A Puppet in the Making*</u>
I'm a puppet in the making
One that laughs and sings
And you can organise me
Make me do your things...

I'm a puppet in the making

With everything that brings
And you're the puppet master
Controlling from the wings...

I'm a puppet in the making
Just waiting for my strings...

Then I would close the book before anyone realised that it hadn't been the poem on the page that I had opened. There would be a polite round of applause and then we would move on with whatever the class was supposed to be about that day. Occasionally someone would bring in one of my father's books and ask me to sign that but I always refused, it wasn't my work and I had no right to put my name to it. Besides, he had been a great poet, an enormous creator of images through words and I had never risen to his high standards.

I never taught my father's work in my classes, it didn't seem appropriate, and of course I never taught my own. I wondered if somewhere in the world there might be an English Lit course which mentioned one of my poems. I wondered what they would say about my famous puppet poem if they were to analyse it? It's not about a puppet, that's easy enough to spot, but what else could they say? That it's about love becoming an obsession, would they see that? I hoped that they would. Would they compare it to my father's work? Would they say that the son didn't have even a tenth of the talent of the father?

It is never easy being the son or daughter of a famous father or mother I'm sure anyone in that situation would say so. For me, being the son of Lyndon Strachan, the poet, had always been hard. Hard from an early age when I realised that I wasn't like all the other kids growing up in a house with a father and a mother, and harder still when I finally dared to take my first fumbling steps into the world of literature.

By the time I was old enough to have memories, say three and a half or four maybe, my father was long gone never to return. At the end of the First World War, being one of the lucky soldier poets who survived, he had been at a bit of a loss for what to do. In the end, he decided to hole up for the winter somewhere sunny to write a second volume of war poems whilst his memories were still vivid. His first, entitled *Where Oblivion Reigns,* after the first poem he had written in the trenches, had been received very well and he was eager to make a career out of poetry. He hoped that going somewhere completely new would also provide him with the inspiration to move him away from just writing war poetry.

<u>Where Oblivion Reigns</u>
A funeral of flesh takes place
Where naked murder has no face,
A cauldron filled with writhing limbs
Where Armageddon ends and death begins.
A killing ground of blood and hail
Where wave upon wave are doomed to fail,
A foreign field of lifeless veins
The naked anguish where oblivion reigns.
The rifles talk with burning tongues
Of when the creeping barrage comes
Through darkened skies of fiery lead
To rain upon the living dead.
There was a time of silken dreams
Of talking corn and whispering streams
The innocent songs of night jars
The calm of cool skies and stars.

I don't know how, because on the rare occasions I actually met him we never got to talk about it, but for reasons unknown he ended up on the Island of Menorca early in 1919. There he rented a little cottage on some cliffs overlooking a beautiful sandy beach. The owner of the cottage sent his young daughter to clean for this new English guest on a daily basis and they quickly fell in love.

My mother told me on many occasions that my father had been the most handsome man she had ever seen and that she had fallen in love with him at first sight. Her name was Soledad, which means loneliness, but my father renamed her Sol which means sun because, according to her version of their story, she was too beautiful to have such a depressing name and she brightened his days like the sun in the Menorcan sky above. She was always known that way from then on. She never went back to being Soledad and she never went back to Menorca either. When her father had found out that she was pregnant he had thrown her out of his house and thrown his worthless tenant out of the little cottage on the cliffs overlooking the beautiful sandy beach.

My father had brought her back to England with him and taken up a job in my grandfather's factory which put food in cans. The factory had prospered in the war years and the family was very well off. My parents were married just before the birth of my brother, Stephen. I came along quickly on his heels.

Stephen Strachan, now there's a poetic-sounding name, okay it's not the masculine war-hero-sounding name of Lyndon Strachan the all-conquering and twice-wounded soldier of Flanders fields, but a romantic poetic name. A name for someone who might have written beautiful scenes of love amidst the poplars or something. He had been a great scholar too.

Yes, my brother Stephen should have been the poet, not me. But, by the time I had reached eighteen and decided to run away to war to find him, he was already dead. He had been lost during the Battle of Jarama and was probably buried in some mass grave that had never been found. Maybe he had been blown up by a shell during the advance through the olive groves and there had been nothing left worth burying. Maybe he had been taken prisoner, during the chaos of retreat, and shot, one cold morning at dawn, his back against the twisted trunk of a gnarled old olive tree.

Had I known that he was dead I would never have gone to war to try to find him, and my life would have been completely different. He was my mother's favourite and I guess I had hoped that by finding him and returning him to her she might love me equally to show her gratitude. She blamed herself for his death.

He had run away to fight in a war for her country. The Island of Menorca had declared itself in support of the Spanish Republic whilst its neighbours, Mallorca and Ibiza, had sided with the Nationalists, and so my brother had joined the Communist party and got himself into Republican Spain to fight against Fascism. I don't know if he intended to go to Menorca and fight there. He had often asked our mother about her family on the island, so possibly he had naively thought that he might go there and join up with our Spanish cousins, but of course he had been hurriedly forced into the International Brigades along with all the other foreign volunteers.

A part of my mother had died with Stephen. There had been a period when she must have feared that both her sons were dead, as I was posted as missing too, for a long time. When I eventually returned she went through the motions of being happy that I had miraculously survived, but I could see it in her eyes, always the same question, why had Stephen been taken and not me? She was never the same again. She became prematurely old and grieved herself to death.

My father came to her funeral. Later back at the house when everyone else had left, he whispered to me that she had been the only woman he had ever truly loved. What a load of crap. There had been so many women that I bet he couldn't even remember the names of half of them.

An hour later he was gone. He drove across town to the huge mansion he shared with his latest female companion. My mother and her poet had never divorced something that had given her a lingering hope that he would one day return to her. But he wasn't the type of man to be tied down. He had left her with two small boys to go off on a grand tour of Italy to find the inspiration he needed to become a great romantic poet, but I think he just wanted to escape the sound of babies crying and the stink of nappies and a creeping feeling of unhappiness.

My mother's funeral had been the last time I had seen him. He had followed my mother a few years later, after a car crash in the Alps, where he had been looking for yet more inspiration. He had driven off the side of a mountain. Maybe he had done it on purpose maybe he had just been driving too fast and had lost control, who knows. I found myself on the receiving end of a large fortune. Most of this came from the money he had inherited from the sale of his father's canning factory. Very little came from the royalties from his books. People didn't buy poetry compilations any more, not even great ones by the great Lyndon Strachan.

I sold his mansion in London, just as I had sold my mother's little two up two down. I remained living in my tiny West London flat just as I had always done. I paid off the mortgage and thought I might take a holiday, but I never got around to it. Anyway, where would I go? The only place I had ever wanted to visit was Spain, but Spain was closed to me. I knew as a former Communist and member of the International Brigades that I would never be allowed to return. If by some miracle I did manage to enter the country there was still the possibility that I might be shot, perhaps my death sentence was still in the files.

Did they have a list of all those who had escaped before a death penalty could be carried out? Were there pictures at all the border crossings just in case one of them tried to slip back into Spain? Probably not, but it was a risk I wasn't going to take. The Franco regime had showed itself to be totally unforgiving. I had heard that Franco's health was failing, but even his death wouldn't necessarily mean that Spain was going to change. Perhaps there would be another civil war or more likely just another military dictator.

At last I managed to snap out of my daydream and focus on the pile of papers on my desk that needed marking. If I didn't start straight away I wouldn't have time to get them finished before my next class. With a heavy heart I picked up my red pen and reached for the first paper on the top of the pile. There was a knock on the door. Shit, just what I didn't need. Who the hell would come knocking on my door during marking time? I toyed with the idea of not answering.

Whoever was out there knocked for a second time. I put down my red pen and got wearily to my feet. It was probably some first year student who was looking for one of my colleagues and had found their office door locked and wanted to know when their professor was normally around. As if I would know.

I opened the door and saw a young woman standing there. She was mid twenties I guessed, slightly older than most of our students.

"Professor Strachan?" she asked. I thought about pointing out the name plate in the middle of the door but in the end I didn't.

"Yes. What can I do for you?"

"My name is Amanda Hales, I'm studying Spanish." She offered me her thin hand to shake. She had the longest, thinnest fingers I had ever seen with long thin fingernails as well. I shook her hand as gently as I could.

"This floor is the English Department," I informed her.

"I know that," she said with a little laugh. "It's you I've come to see."

"Me?"

"Yes."

"You'd better come in then," I decided.

I showed her to a spare chair and sat down behind my desk, moving the pile of unmarked papers across to the other side. I hoped she wouldn't stay long. I had marking to do.

"So, what did you want to see me about?"

"Well, it's like this. I'm doing my final thesis for my Spanish degree and I wanted to do something about the Civil War. I thought perhaps a study on the International Brigades."

"And what's that got to do with me?"

"You were in the International Brigades, weren't you?"

"Who told you that?"

"No one, I was reading a book about the British Brigade in the library and there was a list of names at the back. It said after the name in brackets those who were killed or those who were well-known, you know like Laurie Lee for example. It said Martin Strachan (poet). My roommate is doing a class with you I just put two and two together."

"I see. Sorry but I don't think I can help you. I was only there a few months."

"What I need is a firsthand account. That would really make my paper stand out from the rest. There are several others who are going to do something about the Civil War. I want mine to be the best."

"What can I say? It's just something I don't want to be reminded of."

"Was it that bad?"

"It was terrible. All wars are terrible and civil wars are the worst wars of all."

She quickly opened a little shoulder bag she had brought with her and reached inside feeling for something she knew was there. I hoped she wouldn't break one of her beautiful long nails on my account.

Eventually she found what she was looking for and pulled out one of those spiral bound reporter's notebooks. There was a pencil stuck into the metal spiral and she pulled it out and then opened the notebook.

"I like that. Is it all right if I use that quote in my thesis?" she asked as she quickly scribbled it down. "I'll have to translate it into Spanish of course."

Without thinking I quickly gave her the translation. She looked up from her notebook.

"So you speak Spanish. Did you learn it in the war?"

"No. My mother was Spanish. I was brought up bilingual."

"I see. That must have been a big help when you arrived to fight."

"Actually, being bilingual almost got me killed."

"So tell me about it."

"I said I wasn't going to talk about it remember?"

"Please. You must. My marks haven't been great this year this is my last chance to boost my coursework grade."

"Have you been to Spain?" I asked her.

"Yes. I spent last year in Barcelona. It's a wonderful city, but the people are still so sad after what happened in the war."

"Barcelona was where I arrived in Spain."

"Let's start there then, shall we? Just start at the beginning and tell me all about it."

"It's not easy to talk about," I said. "Anyway, right now I'm kind of busy." I suddenly wanted to be alone. I had thought about what happened to me during the

Civil War a lot, of course I had. I still had nightmares but this was the first time I had ever been asked to talk in detail about it. Even all these years later I wasn't sure I was ready for that, especially with someone I didn't know.

"Do you want me to come back another time when it's more convenient? Tomorrow maybe?"

"I teach all day tomorrow," I lied.

"Well, another time, whatever suits you."

"Let me think about it. Do you have a phone number? Maybe I'll call you."

"Sure." I saw her disappointment in her eyes. She knew I wasn't going to call her. She quickly scribbled a number on her reporter's notepad and tore of the page and handed it to me. She'd written her name Amanda below the number and my bit about terrible civil wars was noted at the top of the page, she obviously thought that it was no longer going to be of any use to her for her thesis.

I walked her to the office door and opened it for her. She offered me her long thin hand to shake once more.

"Thank you for your time," she said politely which made me start to feel bad. "I expect you get people wanting to talk to you about your experiences in the Civil War all the time. It must be a real nuisance."

"Actually you're the first."

She looked surprised.

"By the way, there was a Stephen Strachan on the list of names below yours, any relation?"

"He was my brother."

"It said (killed) after his name."

"That's right."

"I'm sorry," she said as if she now thought she knew why I didn't want to talk about my war in Spain. She turned and left and walked away down the corridor. I watched until she turned a corner and then went back into my office. I picked up her phone number from my desk, screwed it into a tight ball and tossed it onto the waste paper basket. Sitting down I searched for my red pen and worried that I wouldn't get all the papers marked before my next class.

CHAPTER SEVENTEEN

I didn't think anything more about Amanda Hales and her long thin fingers or her Civil War thesis, but a couple of weeks later she knocked again at my office door. I must confess I felt a little guilty upon seeing her there, but she didn't seem annoyed, in fact she seemed excited about something.

"Have you heard the news?" she gushed.

"What news?"

"Franco's dead!"

"Franco? Wow! When did it happen?"

"This morning."

I knew that the Caudillo had been on life support for several weeks, he was even being referred to as Francostein in some newspapers. But now he was dead. What would his death mean for Spain?

"You'd better come in," I told her.

"I don't mean to disturb you."

"It's okay, I'm not doing anything important at the moment."

"Well, if you're sure."

"I was meaning to call you," I said although I guessed she knew it was a lie.

"I've been trying to think about another thesis, but I haven't come up with anything good yet."

"When do you have to hand it in?"

"By the end of next term."

"We don't have much time then."

"You mean you'll do it?"

"If that's what you want. I warn you though I don't think I was there long enough to be of much use to you."

"Wow! A firsthand account, that's really going to give my thesis the edge over the rest. Do me a favour, will you? If anyone else comes to ask you say no, okay?"

"Sure. You have exclusive rights."

"That's great. Wait 'til I tell my mum - she loves your work."

"That's nice."

"I'll bring my camera and take a photo to send her next time, she'll like that."

It was difficult not to get caught up in Amanda's enthusiasm. I just hoped that my meagre memories wouldn't be too much of a disappointment to her. If she was banking on my contribution to her thesis making the difference between passing or failing her degree then she might well be disappointed.

I invited her into my office and she sat down and began to rummage through her bag looking for her notebook. I guess she had been pretty confident that I was going to tell her my story after all.

"Where do you want to start?" I asked her.

"Let's start at the beginning, shall we? Why did you go to Spain? To fight against fascism I suppose."

"No, not at all. I went to try to find my brother Stephen."

*

That night, at home, I decided to have a good sort through of my old photograph albums and documents to see if I could find anything that Amanda might want to use in her work. We didn't take a lot of photos back in the thirties, cameras were expensive and film and developing too of course, and who would take a camera to war with them? I guess there must have been cameramen and reporters in Spain during the Civil War, I knew Ernest Hemmingway had been working there for instance, but I don't remember anyone having taken my picture as a Brigadista. I don't suppose any cameraman in his right mind would have wanted to cross the Ebro with us at that time.

There was a very small photo of my brother and I together in the garden of our house. I guess my mother must have taken it before he marched off to war. It was faded grey and I looked like a sickly kid who was about to cry. There was another one of him on his own, this one preserved in a cheap frame, Stephen looking defiantly at the camera. He seemed so confident, so untouchable. That was the mistake of youth going to war, they felt they were indestructible.

Within a year of that picture having been taken he would be dead.

Then I came a across a photograph of my mother as a young woman. She looked so different from how I had always remembered her. For a while I couldn't put my finger on what it was, but in the end I realised that she looked happy. It must have been before my father left her I concluded. Seeing my mother so young, so beautiful, so unaware of what was going to happen to her perfect little family depressed me. I put down her picture and went to the kitchen to pour myself some scotch.

Drinking was a bad thing for me. I wasn't the kind of person who could just have one glass and then leave it alone. I tried hard enough, but it was stronger than me this overwhelming desire to drink myself into oblivion and it gripped me every night by the throat and shook me hard until I fell to pieces. Some nights I could resist, but only just. Most nights I simply gave in.

*

I showed Amanda the photograph of my brother the next time we met up. I had told her I preferred to meet for a coffee after work rather that in my office during the day. I had things to keep me occupied during work hours it was the long evenings that were hell to get through. I figured that if I was going to help her with her work then it was only right that she should help me to avoid the demons that roamed around my flat in the long winter evenings. We were sat in a little café not far from the university by a large window with a view of a London street in the pouring rain. It was warm enough and quiet too, most people were hurrying straight home umbrellas bent against the wind. It was not the type of night to be going out for coffee.

I watched her handle Stephen's last photograph, at least the last one that I knew of, with her long thin fingers. They were white like marble. Her nails caught the light and flickered as she moved them, they were obviously painted with clear varnish. Maybe that gave them extra strength. I guess she saw me looking.

"I'm a model," she told me. "I let people use my hands for pictures."

"Really?" I asked tearing my eyes away from her hands at last.

"Yes, it helps me pay my way through university."

"So, you're a model but they only want pictures of your hands?"

"Well, I don't think anyone would pay me to take a picture of my face," she said with a laugh.

I looked at her face, you know, really looked at it, as if seeing it for the first time. It was a pretty face. She had lots of pale freckles, very pale, small freckles, lots of them, especially around her eyes. And of course she had that long beautiful auburn hair which was almost curly but not quite and at that moment sparkled because of the raindrops hiding there after our recent mad dash under an inadequate umbrella.

"I can't think why they don't want to take photographs of your face, it's a perfect face." Then I stopped myself. I didn't want her to think that I was being inappropriate or anything. I was in my mid fifties. Maybe I was thirty years older than her. I didn't want her to think that I was coming onto her or something. I didn't want her to feel uncomfortable with me.

"That's kind of you to say Professor," she giggled.

"I'm sorry. I didn't mean… and don't call me professor. My name's Martin."

"I know. It's okay, thank you. No one has ever said I had a perfect face before."

"I like faces," I told her.

"I know. My flat mate lent me your poems the other day and I read *A Hundred Faces*, so I know you like faces."

A Hundred Faces had been the title of my second slim volume of poems and also the title of the first poem in the collection. I guess after the puppet poem it was my best known. For me it was my personal favourite of all the hundreds or thousands that I had written, but then I had written it about someone very special who wasn't in my life for long, but had always been in my life, if you catch my meaning.

<u>A Hundred Faces</u>

I searched for love in unusual places and
I looked for love in a hundred faces.
And the only eyes I ever wanted to see
Were your eyes,
And the only voice I ever wanted to hear
Was your voice,
And the only arms where I could have been safe
Were your arms.

I reached for love but I never could touch it and
I hoped to find calm but only knew fear.
And the only soul I wanted to touch
Was your soul,
And the only praise I ever longed for
Would have been praise from you,
And the only heart I never dared to break
Was your heart.

I searched for love in unusual places and
I looked for love in a hundred faces.

"So, you model your hands, for what exactly?" I asked.
"Well, close up photos mostly for adverts - rings, bracelets, watches that sort of thing. I've also been in a couple of films as a hand extra."
"What does a hand extra have to do?"

"Some actresses might be very beautiful but they might have very ugly hands or bite their finger nails. That's where I come in if a director needs a close up of them drinking wine or smoking or caressing the male actor's chest or running her fingers through his hair."

"Wow! So which famous actors have you caressed?"

"None! They all have chest doubles or hair doubles for that part. I normally work when the film is almost finished and all the famous actors have long gone."

"I see, so it's not as glamorous as it sounds then?"

"It's not glamorous at all, but it pays the rent sometimes."

"Must be tough being a student in London."

"You've no idea."

"And what do you plan to do when you finish your degree?"

"I want to work in films or television, but not as an actress, as a researcher or something like that."

"Sounds good. Sorry Amanda, we came here to talk about Spain and I'm side-tracking you."

"It's okay. If I'm going to dig around in your life I guess you've got every right to dig into mine."

"Where did we get to last time?"

She opened her reporter's notepad to the last thing she had written and thought for a second about something she wanted to know.

"What equipment did you have to carry into battle with you?"

"That's a good question. Let me think. I can only talk about the Battle of the Ebro of course, but we travelled light. We had rifles and some bullets, a blanket, a few had hand grenades but I didn't, they scared the life out of me. I wasn't a good thrower anyway."

"And that's it?"

"More or less. We left our kit bags behind before we moved up to the river. They were supposed to be brought forward to us later. I don't know what happened to mine. Not that I had anything special in it."

"No books? I imagine a poet going to war with a kitbag full of books."

"I wasn't a poet then."

"Didn't you write any poems in Spain?"

"No. You think because my father was a war poet that war would have inspired me to write too, but it didn't. I wasn't there long and I was just a kid."

"When did you write your first poem?"

"When I was in my first year at university. We had this fantastic old lecturer who read poetry in such an enthusiastic way that he made me want to write some myself."

"Did you ever ask your father for advice?"

"No, never."

CHAPTER EIGHTEEN

Slowly, over the course of several weeks Amanda began to fill her notebook with my brief Spanish Civil War escapade. She was patient and good at getting very personal details out of me. I told her about how I had been wounded and how Julia had nursed me back to health. I'd never mentioned the girl to anyone before.

Of course, talking about that time opened up all my old emotional wounds so that I found myself continually reliving those few weeks I had spent in Spain when I was alone at night over and over again. When I finally fell asleep I would have nightmares about the girl's death, and I would wake up with a huge burden of guilt that I knew would take me all day to shake off.

"What happened to Julia?" Amanda asked me one afternoon back at the coffee shop.

"They shot her," I whispered. And then without warning I burst into tears. I hadn't cried about it since I had left Spain so many years before, I had bottled it all up inside and tried to live with it as best I could. The tears ran down my cheeks uncontrollably and I couldn't stop the flow. Amanda leaned across and put her arm around my shoulders.

"I'm sorry," she said.

*

Amanda left me alone for a few days and I began to wonder if she had decided that my story wasn't going to be of any use to her. I went back to going through the motions of life, of waking up at seven and getting the tube to work, of giving lectures and marking essays and getting home and drinking myself to sleep.

Then she was back at the end of a Friday afternoon, full of apologies for having stirred up my memories and asking for forgiveness. She would stop using me for her thesis if I found things too painful to continue. I told her it was okay to continue, I had missed her company, and besides it was probably good to talk about things from that time to try to exorcise the ghosts that had haunted me for so long.

As it was Friday she suggested that we should go to a pub and have a pint rather than to the usual coffee shop. The thought scared me a bit, I wasn't used to drinking in public and I didn't know how I would behave, but in the end I let her persuade me.

The pub was dark and miserable and nearly empty. It smelt of stale smoke and body odour. We sat in a corner and sipped at our beer for a while and then she asked me about how I had escaped from the Fascists after they captured me at the venta. I told her about jumping out of the back of a lorry when the two guards had fallen asleep and about how I had escaped into the forest.

Over a second pint, I told her about crossing the Ebro back to my own side of the lines and about my trial at the military prison in Barcelona.

"So, you were sentenced to death?" she gasped. "How come you survived?"

"Lyndon Strachan."

"Your father?"

"Yep, the great man saved me. My mother sent him over to Spain to fetch his sons back. He only found me. He knew a lot of people in government and pulled the necessary strings and walked into my prison cell and carried me out slung over his shoulder. I was barely conscious. Another day or two and I would have been dead, if they hadn't executed me first."

"Wow, how did he find you?"

"I don't know. Guess he just figured that I wasn't cut out to be a soldier and that a deserters' prison was the obvious place to look."

"And they just let you leave?"

"Lyndon Strachan wasn't the kind of person who took no for an answer. He convinced them that there had been a terrible misunderstanding and that he had come to take his boy home and that was that. We flew to Toulouse where I spent a few weeks in hospital and then when I felt strong again we took a train to Paris."

"So why do I get the impression that you hated your father when he saved your life?"

"Maybe that was why I hated him."

*

A few weeks later Amanda handed me the first draft of her thesis. I corrected a lot of grammatical mistakes in her Spanish for her. I could see why she might be on the borderline between pass and fail. She had done a good job at reproducing my story though, faithfully portraying it for what it was, a terrible folly that had almost cost me my life. I could so easily have become just another foreign Brigadista whose life had been smudged out in Spain. In the book she had found about the British volunteers I could so easily have been Martin Strachan (killed) in the entry above Stephen Strachan (killed).

Instead, I was Martin Strachan (poet). And yet I had never written a single line about the Spanish Civil War, preferring I guess to blot it out of my memory and yet, every love poem I had ever written had been for Julia, seeing as she was the only love I had ever known.

*

Amanda came to find me on the day that final results were posted. She had passed her degree and she was terribly relieved about it. I told her to go off and celebrate with her friends and she gave me a quick peck on the cheek and hurried off. I never expected to see her again.

CHAPTER NINETEEN
London, June 1977

My retirement do at the end of June was a quiet affair. I was going voluntarily before they sacked me. I was fifty-seven but I felt like a hundred and fifty-seven. Numbers had been falling in our department for several years and someone had to go. I did the decent thing and decided to quit. I didn't need a pay off or anything - I had a lot more money than I could ever spend and no one to leave it to.

Towards the end of a few hushed glasses of wine a young woman entered the room. She was the kind of person that turned heads and I recognised her instantly. It was Amanda Hales, the student who had done her thesis about my participation in the Spanish Civil War. She looked quickly around the room, saw where I was and came over.

"Amanda, how nice of you to come," I said and I stretched out my hand in greeting. She gave me her hand which I was glad to see was as long and thin and white as it always had been.

"Martin, congratulations on your retirement," she said. I offered her a glass of wine and she accepted some white crap that the Head of English had got cheap somewhere. I was drinking the red crap and was no longer feeling the pain after four or five glasses. I steered her away from the little group that I had been talking to so that I could get her on her own.

"So, what job have you ended up in?" I asked.

"I'm a researcher for a television production company," she replied with a smile, almost as if to say didn't I tell you that that was what I was going to do.

"Good. I'm so glad you ended up doing what you wanted."

"And you? What are your retirement plans?"

"Don't know really. Haven't given it a lot of thought."

"Going to write some more poetry at last?"

"No, haven't written anything in twenty years, don't suppose I'll start again now."

"That's a shame. You're a great poet Martin, better than your father."

That took me by surprise. No one had ever said I was better than my father before, and whilst she probably didn't mean it, it was nice of her to say it nevertheless.

"So, are you living in London?" I asked in order to steer the conversation away from poetry.

"No, Manchester. That's where the company I work for is based."

"You came all this way just for my retirement do? I'm terribly flattered, but you didn't have to, a phone call would've been fine."

"Well, to be honest I wanted to talk to you about something to do with work. I tried to ring your flat but the number doesn't exist any more apparently."

"No. I had it cut off, no one ever rang."

"Well, yesterday I rang the university and they told me that today was your last day, so I thought I'd surprise you."

"Thank you, you've made my day."

"I never forgot your story."

"It's not much of a story really."

"Oh, but it is. It's the most total antiwar war story I've ever heard."

"I see."

"That's what I wanted to talk to you about. We're doing a series on the Spanish Civil War and I want you to take part."

"Me? I'm not a war hero or anything."

"No, my producer wants to do an overview about the war in Spain, but he wants to interview survivors to give it a more human angle."

"I was only there a few months. I didn't even fire my rifle in anger."

"I'd like to take you back to Spain. That's what the series is all about. We're going to take some of the British Brigadistas back to the battlefields."

"I wasn't in a battle."

"You were in the greatest battle of them all, the Ebro. It's going to be the last programme of the series. The big climax."

"Not sure I should go back to Spain. Both sides wanted to shoot me."

"Things have changed. Didn't you see the elections a fortnight ago?"

"Yes, of course. First democratic elections since the war, doesn't mean I've been forgiven does it?"

"Don't be silly, no one's looking for you now. Franco's dead and buried and Spain is a democracy."

"I'm not sure I'd feel safe there."

"I'll make sure you're safe."

"So you'd come with me?"

"Every step of the way."

"I'm not going to lie. I'm not going to make out I took a major part in the campaign or anything. I'll tell my story and that's it."

"That's what we want. We want to show the individual sacrifices made by very normal people."

"I didn't make any sacrifices."

"Yes you did. You sacrificed your peace of mind. You've been fighting the Spanish Civil War everyday in your mind for nearly forty years."

"If you say so."

"I know so."

"It's the guilt," I said quietly, feeling that tightness around my heart that I always felt when I thought back to that time, which was precisely why I tried not to think about that time, which was why I no longer wrote poetry. Every poem I had ever written had been about my feelings of love for Julia. I had hoped for many, many years that I could write a poem so special that it would make her sacrifice worthwhile, but I'd never managed it. It was simply an impossible goal. So, eventually, I'd given up trying, but that didn't mean I'd forgotten about her, far from it.

CHAPTER TWENTY
Spain, July 1977

I had only flown once before in my life, when my father had rescued me from prison in Barcelona and we had escaped to Toulouse. That had been aboard an ancient Air France aircraft that did the route from French Morocco to Toulouse via Oran, Alicante and Barcelona. Things had certainly changed now.

Amanda sat next to me on the flight and chattered happily about the series they had been shooting in Spain. She had flown back to London to get me, as I had said I wouldn't fly without her. They had made some great programmes she said and they had high hopes for the last one about the Battle of the Ebro. I was terribly worried about disappointing her and her team.

As we approached passport control I found myself shaking slightly, nervous at the thought that I might be stopped and arrested, but the tired-looking official with a cigarette hanging from his mouth just nodded me through. I was back in Spain. Back in Barcelona.

We spent the night in a hotel just off Las Ramblas and went for a long walk around the city in the evening after a small meal. Of course Barcelona was no longer the besieged city that I remembered. The roadblocks and sandbags were gone, shop fronts were no longer boarded up, and the bombed out buildings had been rebuilt. It was a modern and vibrant city that could have been at home anywhere else in Europe.

We had a drink sitting outside in the street and I realised just how much things had changed since my last visit. There were motor vehicles everywhere. The noise of the constant traffic up and down Las Ramblas was incredible, cars, taxis, buses and screaming ambulances and police cars. It was all so unexpected. Before, in the final months prior to the capture of Barcelona by the Nationalists, motor transport was the exclusive reserve of the armed forces. It was commonplace to see horses and carts moving things around the city and donkeys bringing in produce from the fields to sell at the market.

That night in the hotel I lay awake listening to the noise of the city. Such an impression it had made on me. I was worried about what this trip had in store. Spain had remained cocooned in my mind back in the 1930s, but I now had to come to terms with the fact that, despite the Dictatorship, things had changed completely. The Spain I had known was war-torn Republican Spain on the verge of defeat following its last forlorn throw of the dice. The meal Amanda and I had eaten would have been unthinkable back then. I had been grateful for slops that a pig might reject today.

The one thing I'd never forgotten was the hunger of Spain. I had appreciated every meal I had eaten since, even a simple sandwich, because I knew there had been a time when I was fading away from hunger. I guess that was why I wore a few extra pounds around my waist, it was my body's way of making sure I never faced malnutrition again. I never left anything on my plate at the end of a meal, I ate everything. I even gnawed at meat bones when I had eaten so much that I felt sick.

I hadn't known the Years of Hunger that had followed the Civil War, but it must have been a terrible time, especially in the defeated zones. Now things looked to have improved and the busy Ramblas with its flower stalls and bustling cafés was proof of that.

*

The next day, we took the train to Tarragona and were picked up by the one of the production crew in a rented SEAT 124. The rest of the crew were staying in Miravet on the Ebro. It took us just over an hour and a half to get there. The great castle at Miravet was one of the iconic images of the Battle of the Ebro as photographs were taken there of Republican troops wading across the river at the start of the great adventure.

That night in the dining room of our little hotel I was interviewed by the producer, Mike, on camera for the first time. I was nervous as hell at the start, but he was soft-spoken and kind and I soon relaxed. He asked me how I had crossed the Ebro, and I told him about the wooden boats we had used. Amanda had obviously briefed him on what exactly I could help them with and I talked about the minimal equipment we had taken across with us so that we wouldn't be slowed down on the other side. I then told him that we had set off walking away from the river in the direction of Corbera de Ebro which was our first objective. We were then expected to push on to Gandesa.

*

The journey from Miravet to Gandesa the following morning didn't take long. We approached the town through the Sierra de Pandols and found it brown and red-roofed, tucked in a depression between the hills. It was one of those hills that the crew had come to film. The infamous Hill 481 which was attacked by the British Battalion on 1st August 1938 when the siege of Gandesa was just beginning. They had taken heavy casualties, but I of course hadn't been there with them.

In the afternoon, we went to Corbera de Ebro. It was strange to be able to get there so easily now when it had been impossible for me to get there before. We found that the old town up on the hill had been left in ruins and the camera crew had a visual feast at their disposal. Here were real images of the destructive power of the war, little streets of bombed-out houses, half-destroyed façades with rubble interiors.

They filmed me walking slowly up the hill through the wasted houses although I don't know why. Perhaps they just wanted me to feel a part of what they were doing seeing as they had made me come such a long way. I didn't think that I had been much use to them. I spent the rest of the afternoon hiding from the oppressive heat, keeping myself to myself with my own thoughts. I wondered what it had been like for my fellow brigadistas fighting their way into this little hill town. I probably wouldn't have been much use to them even if I had managed to get there.

I sat on a rock in the shade of a leaning stone wall that was all that remained of someone's house. And I thought about Julia. I should have walked away from the venta when I had the chance. I found myself gently rubbing the scar on my forehead as I often did in times of stress or worry.

"Are you all right?" came Amanda's voice interrupting my thoughts.

"Sure," I replied.

"Have you got a headache from the sun?"

"No, it's just a bit overwhelming to finally be here I guess."

"Of course. Listen, I'm sorry it's taking so long it's just that the producer thinks this is a great place. It's almost as if the war was here yesterday."

"I'm in no hurry," I told her.

"I wanted to show you something," she said taking a folded map out of the pocket of her shorts. She opened it out and spread it carefully across the rock where I was sitting. "I think I've found the crossroads where you were wounded."

CHAPTER TWENTY-ONE

She showed me on her map where two tiny roads crossed on the edge of the Sierra Caballs.
"There was nothing on the maps we were using to plan all this in England, but in Miravet I bought this one and it shows a lot more detail. What do you think?"
"Could be I guess, I don't know."
"We're going to take you there, when we finish up here."
"Why?"
"That's what the series is all about, taking people back to where important things happened to them."
"Just so you can see a man cry like a baby?"
"It's not about that Martin, it's about you putting your demons to rest, finally letting go of the past."
"I aint gonna cry on camera for you."
"You don't have to."
"Shit! You've been using me haven't you? This was all about getting me back to Spain and filming me cracking up."
"Nothing of the sort."
"Bollocks!"
"Martin!"
"Fuck Amanda, do you like seeing grown men cry?"

"I wanted you to find peace. Some of the others thought coming back helped them a lot."

"After they cried for you on camera?"

"Martin please, calm down. We won't film you crying if that's what you want."

"I don't want to go there."

"Please, you have to. I promised Mike that this would be the big climax of the whole series."

"Yeah, right. Am I the only one who got his girlfriend killed? The only one likely to lose it for national TV?"

"I'm sorry you feel that way," she sniffed and I noticed she was crying.

"What do you want from me?"

"I don't want anything from you. You've already done plenty for me. I just wanted to do something for you."

"Like what exactly?"

"Like getting you to say goodbye to Julia so that you can start to live again. Don't you think you've punished yourself enough?"

"I'm a puppet in the making."

"What?"

"I'm a puppet in the making. It was the closest I got to saying goodbye to Julia." I held my head in my hands and wept quietly. Amanda put her arm around me.

"What do you mean?"

"I wanted to write that one great monumental poem that would do her justice, and the puppet was the closest I got. I guess I'm still waiting for my strings, I guess I always will be."

"I didn't know it was about her."

"Everything I wrote was about her. Nothing was good enough. I failed her when I was a kid and I failed her as an adult."

"So A Hundred Faces was for her too?"

"Of course."

"And The Sweetest Pain."

"Yes that too." The Sweetest Pain was the title poem of my third and last poetry collection. The only thing that ever got published after that was Collected Poems which was just a publisher's rehash to try to make a little extra money when their number one living poet ran out of poems.

THE SWEETEST PAIN

You gave me the gift of the sweetest pain
And I've carried it with me for all of my life.
And I never hated you
Not for one moment.
You broke me into a thousand pieces and
No one could ever put me back together.
And I'd let you do it again
(You know I would).

You gave me the gift of the sweetest pain
The purest, greatest gift I ever received.
And I've cherished it and nurtured it and kept it alive.
And in return
What did I give you?
My pride and my youth and a love without shame.
You gave me the gift of the sweetest pain
And I will carry it with me for all of my life…

 "I think you did enough Martin. You immortalised her in three books of poems. No man could have done more."

 "Maybe if I go there and read my poems to her it will help a bit."

 "Yes, let's do that. I think that would be a nice ending for the series."

CHAPTER TWENTY-TWO

We got back into the cars and headed away from Corbera de Ebro. I hadn't enjoyed being there, seeing it so smashed and ruined. I wondered if Amanda really had found the little crossroads where I had been wounded. I peered through the front windscreen from my place in the back hoping to see something familiar. In the Civil War I had arrived at the crossroads from the other direction of course and on foot. Besides, the road was now made of tarmac and wasn't the track I would have known.

Up ahead I saw a small hill and felt my heart skip a beat. I knew without even having to think about it that it was the hill that had overlooked the venta.

"This is the right direction," I said to Amanda who was sitting beside me. She reached across and held my hand. I looked at her face and saw that she was almost as nervous as I was.

We rounded a sharp corner at the bottom of the hill and there was the venta right where I had remembered it. I stared at it in shock. I had never thought we would find anything there. I still pictured just piles of rubble in my mind. But there it was, the walls had been rebuilt, the roof replaced and the big red letters of Venta El Angel had been repainted on the front, exactly as they had been all those years before. It was just like walking back in time.

The cameraman, Rob, who was driving our car, pulled over and stopped at the roadside. My mouth was dry and my heart pounding, I felt more scared than ever before in my life. I got out and just stood and looked at the venta there before me.

"It's open. Would you like to go in?" asked Amanda.

I couldn't speak so I just nodded. We walked across the road over to the door. I was aware of Rob to the side with his heavy camera filming me and Mike getting out of the other car to follow us. So this was their big climax, the unexpected ending for their programme, the Venta El Angel restored to all its former glory.

Amanda pushed down on the handle and held the door open for me to go ahead. And so I walked into that place for the first time in nearly forty years. The dining room was a lot brighter than I had expected but just as small as it always had been. There were wooden tables and chairs and the bar was still at the far side. A group of old men were playing cards and ignoring a small TV on a shelf above them.

I stood there just inside the door and wondered what to do. What did the crew expect from me now? It wasn't what I had always thought I would find when I had returned here in my imagination. It was so perfectly devoid of all the scars from that time, almost as the war had never happened.

A woman emerged from the door to the kitchen wiping her hands on a tea towel. She looked confused to see a group of foreigners huddled together by the door and the camera must have shocked her too. She started to walk towards us.

"Oh god!" I heard myself say although I hadn't been aware of speaking.

"What is it?" asked Amanda.

"Her face."

Her face was striking. It was the sort of face you had to look twice at. It was dominated by her long thin nose, but it was the eyes that drew you in, deep brown, almond-shaped. I knew those eyes, my heart knew those eyes.

"Can I help you?" asked the woman. "Would you like me to prepare a table?"

"You're Julia's daughter, aren't you?" I asked her although I was sure of the answer.

The woman looked at me in a state of total disbelief. How could someone she had never seen before, a foreigner that she had never seen before just walk into the venta out of the blue and mention her mother?

"You know my mother?"

"Is she alive?"

"Of course she is. Why would you say that? Who are you?" I guess it must have been really confusing for her at that moment.

"Where is she?"

"In the kitchen." She turned and called out "Mamá, there's a man here says he knows you." I pushed past her across the dining room, stumbling between the chairs in my haste to reach the kitchen door. But before I could get there Julia emerged. I froze on the spot and just looked at her and she stared back as if she had seen a ghost. Sure we had both changed beyond all recognition, but there was something deep in my heart that leapt with the joy of seeing her alive and she must have felt it too. She raced towards me and threw her arms around my neck.

"Martin," she whispered.

I held her so tightly that I thought I would never be able to let her go. I felt her slight body trembling against me and knew she was crying. And I was crying too.

She pulled back from me just a bit and looked into my eyes, searching my soul as she always had done, just checking to make sure it really was me I guess.

"I promised I'd come back," I told her, it was the only thing I could think of to say to her at that moment.

"You took your time," she responded with a smile.

"I thought you were dead."

"I thought you were dead too."

After a few minutes of just standing together looking at each other, Julia glanced over at the others by the door. Rob was filming us and Amanda was crying. Julia's daughter was just looking at us in disbelief.

"There's someone I need to introduce you to," whispered Julia.

"Your daughter, right?"

"She's your daughter too."

"Mine?"

"Yeah. I found out I was pregnant not long after they took you."

"Jesus!"

She turned me around and led me over to the woman who I now knew to be my daughter.

"Martina, this is your father," she said.

"Martina?" I said in disbelief.

"I named her after you," whispered Julia.

For a second I didn't know what to do, I was in such a state of shock, and then I just reached out and my daughter came into my arms and I held her tight. We were both crying and I didn't care that Rob was filming me, I didn't care at all.

CHAPTER TWENTY-THREE

The production crew sat together at a big table and tucked into a pot of bean stew that Martina brought out from the kitchen for them. She made sure they had plenty of beer too and then came to sit with her mother and I at another table where we could be more private.

While our daughter had been looking after the crew, Julia and I had been finding out how the other had survived. I told her about throwing myself from the fascist lorry that took me away and escaping into the forest. I told her how I had crossed the Ebro back to the Republican side and how my father had turned up in Barcelona and rescued me from prison when I was close to death.

Julia's survival had been simpler she said. Alfonso, her crippled neighbour, had brought the Fascists to get me on the understanding that she would be spared. He thought that with me gone she would eventually agree to marry him.

"Did you marry him?" I asked as our daughter sat down beside me and took my hand.

"No, of course not. I could never have married him. He lost interest when he saw I was pregnant anyway."

"And he didn't try to get you arrested?"

"He died that last winter of war, a lot of people did. Times were tough."

"So, do you have a husband?" I asked cautiously, terribly afraid of the answer.

"No, I never wanted one. What about you? Are you married?"

I shook my head.

"Who'd have me?" I said. Julia smiled at that and reached out to touch the scar on my forehead.

"We were so young," she said.

"We haven't changed," I told her, "not inside."

*

It was well after midnight when the crew decided they ought to get back to the hotel in Miravet. Amanda got up and came over to us. She had a huge smile on her face.

"We ought to get going," she said to me.

"I guess so," I reluctantly agreed. "Thank you Amanda, you know, for this."

"My pleasure," she replied and she walked away back to the others who were starting to collect their things.

"It's time to go," I said to Julia.

"Will you come back?" she wanted to know. She had an anxious look on her face like I was just going to disappear again or something.

"What time do you open for lunch tomorrow?"

"We open for breakfast," said Martina, "at eight."

"See you for breakfast then," I told them. I hugged my beautiful daughter, still finding it hard to believe that she was real, and then Julia came with me outside to where the cars were waiting. I hugged her to me once more.

"I missed you," I told her.

"I know," she said.

*

Early the next morning, Amanda Rob and Mike accompanied me back to the venta. It was our last day in Spain and the rest of the crew had gone to film some other parts of the river, but Mike wanted to do a final interview with Julia and I together with our daughter, the daughter I had never known existed.

After breakfast, at around ten, the venta emptied and I sat with Julia and Martina and put Mike's questions to them in Spanish. He wanted to know what had happened immediately after I had been taken away by the Fascists. Julia told us that Alfonso had walked with her back to her aunt's little farm in the hills and explained to her father that she had almost been arrested for helping a wounded enemy soldier. Her father had thanked him for saving his daughter's life and when Alfonso had left he had exploded with rage.

When he found out a few months later that she was pregnant he wanted to throw her out, but her aunt had said that it was her place and she wasn't about to throw her pregnant niece out. When the baby was born

Julia's father fell in love with her and spoilt her rotten for the rest of his life.

His next question was about the venta. When was it rebuilt? Julia explained in a sad tone that about five years after the end of the war they had a terribly hard winter and her aunt and cousin, Miguelito, both died of pneumonia. Her father decided to sell the farm to their neighbour and used the money to rebuild the Venta El Angel. Julia and her daughter had lived there ever since. They didn't make much of a living said Martina, but they were happy.

"What did you do Martin, I mean when you got back from Spain?" Julia asked me.

"Well, when I got back we were on the verge of war with Germany. Because I had been a member of the Communist Party in order to get into Spain I had a lot of problems trying to get into the armed forces, so in the end I joined the merchant navy and worked on the Atlantic convoys."

"And after the war?"

"I finally went to university and started to write poetry."

"You're a poet?" she asked.

"Not really, at least not any more."

Amanda who had been standing close by listening to us suddenly got up and went across to her bag which was hanging on the back of a chair. She rummaged around inside and came back with a dog-eared copy of my collected poems. She handed it to Julia.

"This is his. He told me that every poem he ever wrote was for you."

"Really?" asked Julia turning to look at me. I nodded dumbly. "Read one for me," she said.

"It's in English," I told her.

"That's okay, you can translate it when you finish."

I opened the book at a random page and for the first time ever, I swear, it opened to A Puppet in the Making. It was the poem I had been going to give her anyway. When I finished I quickly translated the words for her and she hugged me tightly.

"I love you," she whispered.

"I know," I whispered back.

"Are all these poems really for me?" she asked.

"I wrote three books of poems for you," I told her.

"Why so many?"

"Because I never forgot you."

CHAPTER TWENTY-FOUR

We had lunch at the venta. I stood in the kitchen and watched Julia preparing the food whilst the others snacked on olives and cheese and drank wine. When it was ready we all sat down to eat together, there were only a couple of passing travellers at other tables so there wasn't much for Martina to do.

When lunchtime was over, the crew decided to head back to the hotel to get some rest. I stayed behind. Martina left us alone together and disappeared upstairs. Julia and I went and sat out in the patio in the shade of a lemon tree. I didn't like to ask if it was the same tree from before, I preferred to think that it was. The little well was still there too.

"I often come and sit here," she told me, "I always felt close to you here, it's my special place."

"Do you remember when you turned up and I was in the bath tub?" I laughed.

"How could I forget? The bathtub's still down in the cellar I think. Shall I go get it?"

"It's all right. I had a shower this morning. Besides, I don't think I'd fit in that tub any more."

"You sure you don't want to try?"

"You just want to see me naked, don't you?"

She laughed.

"You were so funny back then."

"Was I?"

"Yes. We laughed a lot."

"Despite the war."

"Yes, despite the war."

There was a silence for a while as we both thought back to those distant moments we had spent together in that patio so very long ago, and yet it all seemed so clear, at least to me.

"I'm sorry I couldn't be there when Martina was born."

"You were there. You were always with me."

"Thank you. It must have been tough having a child at that time."

"You have no idea."

I leaned over to kiss her, I'd been waiting to do it since the moment I'd seen her again, and I couldn't wait any longer. It was the first time our lips had touched since our last night together in the cellar all those years before, and yet there was still electricity and excitement like there always had been.

"I'm not sure we should do this," she whispered when we had kissed for about ten minutes.

"Why?"

"You're leaving tomorrow."

"Am I?"

"Aren't you?"

"Only if no one asks me to stay."

"Do you need to be asked?"

"Yes."

"Haven't you got a job and a house and friends and all that stuff to go back to?"

"No. I gave up my job, I hate my flat and I don't have any friends."

"And what will you do here?"

"Buy a little farm."

"A farm?"

"Yes, I always thought we would live on a farm together."

"Do you know anything about farming?"

"No. But you do. You can teach me."

"And what about the venta?"

"Let Martina have it."

"So we just buy a farm, just like that?"

"Yes, just like that. I was thinking of your aunt's farm."

"People live there, they bought it when Alfonso's father died."

"We'll make them an offer they can't refuse."

"I don't have any money."

"It doesn't matter. I've got plenty and I never had anything to spend it on before."

"What makes you think that you can just come and live here with no problems? Do you honestly think we can make a life together after all this time?"

"I've spent nearly forty years living without you and I've been really miserable. I hated every single day. I want to try to get to know you again, to make up for wasted time. If you ask me I'll stay."

"Stay," she said quietly.

CHAPTER TWENTY-FIVE
Madrid, November, 1996

Julia held my hand as the train came to a halt. I wasn't well, I hadn't been for several months, but I didn't want to miss this for anything in the world. I had never been to Madrid before, in fact apart from a couple of trips back to London to sell my house and arrange for a few of my personal possessions to be shipped over, I had hardly left the area around our little forgotten farm tucked between the hills on the edge of the Sierra Caballs. I have to admit I was a terrible farmer. The animals all hated me and everything I planted died, even the fruit trees that had grown there for generations resented my presence, but it didn't matter. I had found peace.

We had two grandchildren because not long after we moved into the farm Martina admitted she was in love with a man from Gandesa and they married and ran the venta together. Julia and I would go there to see them nearly every day and whilst I played with the kids she would help out in the kitchen.

I've never written another poem. I guess I felt I didn't have to. I had wanted to make a big tribute to my lost love, but seeing as I had found her again it was no longer necessary. I could tell her how special she was everyday, and I still do.

We checked into our hotel off the Gran Via and rested for a while, the journey had tired me out. Julia lay beside me on the bed and I listened to her breathing. I still found it hard to believe that we were together again and I never tired of being with her. If we ever argued, which was rare, one of us would quickly remind the other that we were so lucky to have each other and whatever had caused the argument would just fade away.

I hated being ill. I hated the thought that one day, perhaps in the not too distant future I was no longer going to be by her side. She had believed that I had died once before and she had never forgotten me. I knew that if I went before her she would keep me with her in her heart just as she had always done.

The next morning, I dressed in my new suit and Julia put on her new dress and we waited down in the lobby for the taxi. When we got to the reception I was surprised to see so many others there. Someone told me that 350 old Brigadistas had come back to Spain from all over the world. Of course I knew no one and no one knew me, but we all talked together in little groups and our wives talked together too. There were several like me who had decided to make their homes in Spain and others who had married Spanish women they had met in later life. There were speeches about blood and sacrifice and of course I thought about my brother Stephen when we drank a toast to fallen comrades. What a waste of so many young lives. Not just international volunteers and not just soldiers but everyone who had perished because of the war, either while it lasted or during the reprisals that followed. I was glad that Spain had found peace.

We were all given Spanish nationality, just as we had been promised by the leaders of the Republic so many years before. I took my new passport and sat back down at the table next to Julia. I saw she was crying. I smiled at her and wiped a tear away from her cheek.

"I love you," I whispered.

"I know," she said.

ALSO BY KELVIN HUGHES
THE LAST LORRY

NUMBER 1 BESTSELLER IN HISTORY OF SPAIN ON
amazon.co.uk

Madrid. March 1939.

The final hours of the Spanish Republic.

As the doomed Spanish capital prepares to surrender after two years of stubborn resistance, one final mission remains. A lorry, disguised as an ambulance, must leave the city and head south to the port of Alicante, where a ship is waiting to take its valuable secret cargo to South America. The lorry's cargo is so important that the victorious rebels will stop at nothing to capture it.

The person given this unenviable task is a young Captain, Daniel Miller Gonzalez, a man who has proved his loyalty to the legitimate Government of Spain on battlefields across the Iberian Peninsula. Together with his lifelong friend Fernando, an English nurse, and the driver of the lorry, Dani tries to outwit the advancing forces of General Franco in a dangerous game of cat and mouse along the last remaining route south out of Madrid. He knows that this final corridor of escape is closing in on him and that every moment is vital, but they can only travel along the back roads and at night as Rebel aircraft are out hunting for them during the daytime.

The man entrusted with the task of hunting down the last lorry is the ruthless Captain Roberto Ruiz Roman, a brutal and sadistic expert in extracting information and sniffing out 'Reds.' And, as General Franco himself has said "better Dead than Red." Captain Ruiz has the entire rebel war machine at his disposal for this final wartime mission, and he is not a man accustomed to failure.

This is a story of supreme loyalty, of courage when all hope is lost, and, ultimately, of betrayal.

ALSO BY KELVIN HUGHES
THE FORGOTTEN FOOTBALLER

I'd had a spectacular career. I'd won three league titles with Arsenal and played nearly fifty games for my country, over half of them as captain, but I had never been involved with a team of no-hopers before.

Let me explain. After serving seven years of a ten year prison sentence I tried to get a job in football when I was released, any job. But no one would have me. I spent six months applying for every football position that came up. Most clubs didn't bother to call me back. I couldn't even get an interview for the job of tea boy. That's when I thought I should go back to my roots and start off at the bottom again. My first team had been Sheppey United and when I was sixteen I had played for them in the Southern League, so I rang up the Chairman and was surprised to be given the chance to become their new Manager. I didn't even know there wasn't already a manager I just thought I could help out with training, maybe with the youth team or the reserves.

I didn't know that Sheppey United were in as bad a way as I was. The previous season they had been relegated from the Kent League Premier Division without winning a single game. Now they were in the Kent League Division One (East), they had no ground and a large outstanding debt. If the truth be told we probably needed each other or maybe even deserved each other.

So I moved back to Sittingbourne where I had spent my childhood and tried to set about rebuilding my life after over twenty years away. It wasn't going to be easy, I knew that. And then I bumped into Christine who had been my first love, my only love, and things started to get really complicated.

ALSO BY KELVIN HUGHES
THE TALLEST TOWER

Bologna, 1219

A marriage is arranged between Fabio Richi and Giulietta Catalani and the families agree to build two towers, almost within touching distance, to represent the union. The wedding date is set for Christmas Day 1222 and so the race is on to get both towers completed in time.

Bologna is a prosperous city state, its skyline cluttered with strange towers built by all the leading families. Signore Leonardo Richi decides that his tower will be the tallest and appoints the city's leading architect to take control of the build. He also has plans to take over control of the City Council and has the help of his evil Protector, Massimo Marinelli. His main rival is his own brother Cardinale Pietro, the Bishop of Bologna.

Bologna is suddenly sent into decline by a series of earthquakes and successive poor harvests. When the population is on the verge of starvation, the people look for a strong leader to help them survive and to restore the city to its former glory. Which of the Richi brothers will emerge to fill the power vacuum?

As her wedding approaches, Giulietta finds herself falling in love with Luca the son of the builder in charge of the Catalani Tower. How can she marry Fabio Richi when her heart belongs to another?

This is a story of ruthless ambition, of a passionate and forbidden love and, most of all, the story of the tallest tower ever built in the city of Bologna.

POETRY BY KELVIN HUGHES
A SPITFIRE IN THE CLOUDS

I started the search for the perfect poem a long time ago now.
I was in my late teens I think.
I just suddenly felt inspired by everything around me. I was fortunate that at that time I had the opportunity to live in two different countries as part of my studies. My senses were bombarded by new sights and experiences and of course new sounds as I fought with two foreign languages. I think being immersed first in French and then in Spanish also gave me a greater appreciation for my own language and I started to experiment in poetry.

I must have been writing something new nearly every day, as I have boxes of verses written on scraps of paper of all colours and all shapes and sizes. This collection really is just a selection. I left out so much. Early poems that have survived the test of time for me include THE LADY AND THE SOLDIER which I wrote in the back of a car passing through a tiny French village in the Pyrenees when I saw a war memorial and also FORGOTTEN TOWN about an abandoned village that had been flooded for the construction of a dam again in the Pyrenees. From my time in Spain in 1988-89 THE CITY OF THE SEA about the beautiful city of Cadiz is here.

More modern offerings have been inspired by my move to Spain, COUPLE IN A DOORWAY for example and of course by my children – I have included one for each of them; DAVID AND I UP ON THE ROOF and SANDRA THE BUTTERFLY PRINCESS. Who doesn't feel inspired by their children? And for my wife? I wrote A WORLD OF A HUNDRED AND ONE RAINBOWS for her a long time ago now, I couldn't decide if I wanted to be a matador or a poet. Which would impress her most? In the end she got the poet...

I grew up in Kent and over the years I have revisited it many times in poetry; OVER MEDWAY WATERS PASSING NOW, A WHITE HORSE and LYING UNDER THE CHERRY TREES are all included. Which brings me, finally to my latest poem and the title for this collection: A SPITFIRE IN THE CLOUDS which I wrote for the 75th anniversary of the Battle of Britain a lot of which took place in the skies above the Garden of England.

Did I find the perfect poem somewhere along the way? I hope not because that would mean the end of the search and I would like to think that every now and then I will still feel inspired to put down something in verse… the search goes on.

MY WEBSITE IS: kelvinhughesauthor.wix.com/author-blog

Follow me on FaceBook: kelvin hughes - writer